The New Girl & the Chestnut Mare

A new girl arrives at Saddle Creek and bonds with a misunderstood chestnut mare, sparking friendships, rivalries, and her first real show.

The Saddle Creek Riders

Book 1

Wren Willowbrook

Chapter One

Emma Hayes pressed her forehead against the cool car window as the highway curved toward the mountains. She watched the scenery change for the hundredth time: from the flat stretches of her old hometown to the rolling hills of what would soon - too soon - become her new one. Golden grasses bent in the wind, distant barns dotted the fields, and the sky opened wide above everything like it had nothing to hide. It was beautiful. Annoyingly beautiful. And Emma wished she didn't have to see any of it.

Her parents talked quietly in the front seats, their voices little more than background noise under the hum of tires. About jobs and boxes still needing to be unpacked, about how the movers had scratched the dresser, and whether the new water heater would actually hold up. Grown-up things. Practical things. None of them the things that mattered to Emma.

Like the fact that she had left her entire life behind yesterday morning - her school, her best friend Nora, her soccer team, the small ice-cream shop where she'd spent practically every Saturday - and now here she was, driving toward a place she didn't know, filled with people she didn't know. And horses.

Well... the horses *were* the one potential upside.

Her mom glanced back from the passenger seat. "How are you holding up, sweetheart?"

Emma pulled away from the window and shrugged. "Fine."

But she didn't feel fine. She felt like someone had scooped out her insides and left behind a hollow space where her excitement should be.

Her dad tried a cheerful tone. "We're almost there. About fifteen minutes now. Saddle Creek's supposed to have amazing trails. Your mom saw pictures."

Her mom nodded. "Trails, mountains, forests. And that riding stable I told you about. We drove past it briefly on the house-hunting trip. Looked like something straight out of a storybook."

Emma forced a smile, but it felt thin. Her mom had told her all about Saddle Creek Stables. How friendly everyone was. How beautiful the horses were. How they offered beginner lessons and weekend events and—according to one overly enthusiastic brochure - "adventures waiting around every bend."

None of that changed the fact that she hadn't asked to move.

Outside, the road narrowed and dipped into a valley dotted with tall pines. A sign appeared, painted white with neat green letters:

WELCOME TO SADDLE CREEK - WHERE EVERY PATH LEADS TO SOMETHING NEW

Emma sighed. "That sounds like something for a tourist brochure."

Her dad chuckled. "You have to admit, it's a pretty sign."

Emma didn't want to admit it. But she did notice the carved horses at the bottom of the post - three of them running side by side, manes flying. Someone had put love into the design. Someone who cared about horses. Maybe everyone here did.

The road straightened again, passing a grocery store, a gas station, and a café called *The Giddy Up Grill.* A mural covered one wall: a group of riders crossing a meadow at sunset. The art was warm, bright, confident - everything Emma wasn't feeling.

"See?" her dad said. "Horse country."

Emma's mom tapped the window lightly. "And look - there are stables just ahead."

Emma lifted her gaze. On the right, a long stretch of white fencing lined a gently sloping pasture. Beyond it, a cluster of red-roofed barns sat at the base of a wooded hill. Several horses grazed in the grass, their tails swishing in the late-afternoon breeze.

But it was the one near the fence that caught Emma's eye.

A chestnut mare stood apart from the others, her coat gleaming like polished copper. She lifted her head as the car approached, ears pricked sharply forward. It was as if she sensed Emma's gaze - like she was looking *straight at her*.

Emma's breath hitched. For a moment the hollow feeling in her chest tightened, then twisted into something else - something unfamiliar and warm. The mare stepped forward a single pace, muscles rippling beneath her coat.

Then the car passed her.

Emma twisted in her seat, craning to keep the mare in view until the fencing disappeared behind a curve of trees.

Her mom noticed. "Beautiful, isn't she? I think that might be Saddle Creek Stables."

Emma nodded, still staring at the empty stretch of road behind them. Beautiful didn't even begin to describe that horse.

"Maybe," her mom continued carefully, "we could go by this weekend. Just to look around. No pressure."

Emma bit her lip. She didn't trust her voice, so she said nothing.

They turned onto Pine Hollow Road, a quieter street lined with big shady maples. Birds hopped along the branches. A few kids rode bikes in the distance. Everything looked calm, peaceful, predictable - like nothing bad had ever happened here.

The car slowed near a beige two-story house with blue shutters and a porch swing.

"Home sweet home," her dad said softly.

Emma didn't get out right away. She looked up at the house - her new house - and felt the ache swell again. She remembered the old one: the scratched banister she and Nora had turned into a mini slide; the window seat she'd filled with pillows; the wall where her height had been marked every birthday. She wondered if the new owners had already painted over the pencil marks.

Her mom came around to open Emma's door. "Let's take a quick look inside before dinner. Maybe we can claim your room before your dad fills it with boxes."

Emma forced a small laugh and stepped out. The breeze carried a faint scent of pine needles and something else - something sweet and earthy. She glanced around, trying to place it.

Her mom breathed in deeply. "I love the smell here. It's so fresh."

Emma wasn't sure how she felt about it. It was different, like everything else.

Inside, the house smelled faintly of cleaning spray and freshly delivered cardboard. The walls were bare. The floors were dusty from movers' footprints. But sunlight streamed through the windows, giving everything a soft, golden glow.

Her dad straightened a stack of boxes. "Your room is upstairs, second on the left. We figured you'd want to set it up your way."

Emma climbed the staircase slowly, her hand sliding along the smooth wooden railing. The second room had a slanted ceiling and a window overlooking the backyard, where tall pines formed a green backdrop against a pale sunset.

She placed her backpack on the carpet and stood quietly, listening to the distant murmurs of her parents' voices downstairs. She'd imagined this moment for months - moving day. She'd imagined it being awful. But somehow it felt even heavier in reality.

She crossed to the window and pressed her palms to the glass. The yard sloped downward toward the tree line, where shadows grew thick between the trunks. A faint sound drifted from somewhere beyond the trees - something high-pitched, almost like a soft whinny carried on the wind.

Emma blinked, leaning closer. But the sound faded, replaced by the whisper of leaves.

Her mom called from downstairs. "Emma? Want to come see the kitchen? We found the plates!"

"Coming," Emma called back, though her gaze lingered on the woods a little longer. Something tugged at her - curiosity, maybe. Or something else entirely.

She turned away and went downstairs.

Dinner was takeout pizza perched on half-unpacked boxes. Her parents chatted excitedly about paint colors, weekend plans, and how many vegetables they could plant in the oversized backyard. Emma poked at her food, offering polite nods and half-smiles whenever one of them looked her way.

Afterward, her dad headed outside to check on the car, while her mom sorted through kitchen boxes. Emma wandered to the front porch, where the cool evening air met her like a soft blanket. The breeze rustled the maple leaves overhead. A pair of crickets tuned up near the steps.

The town was quiet. Not eerily quiet - just soft in a way Emma wasn't used to.

Across the road, an older man was filling a watering can beside his garden. He gave her a friendly wave. "Evening!"

Emma waved back hesitantly. "Hi."

"You must be the new folks in the Hayes place," he said, walking toward the edge of his driveway. His white beard glowed in the porch light. "Name's Mr. Parker. Been here longer than the trees."

Emma smiled politely. "Nice to meet you."

"Your mom told me you like horses," he continued, leaning on his watering can. "We get plenty of them around here. Saddle Creek Stables is just down the road."

Emma perked up a little. "Yeah. We passed it on the way in."

Mr. Parker's eyes twinkled. "Ah, then you probably saw that pretty chestnut mare. Willow."

Willow. The name settled in Emma's mind like a warm stone.

"She's a spirited one," he added. "Belongs to the stable, but she's... particular about people. Funny thing, though." He scratched his beard thoughtfully. "She's been restless lately. The horses get skittish when the nights turn cold. And there've been... noises out by Crestwood Trail."

Emma tilted her head. "Noises?"

"Nothing to worry about," he said quickly. "Probably raccoons. Or one of the ranchers working late. But the woods carry sound strange this time of year." He lowered his voice slightly, as if sharing a secret. "If you ever go riding, stay on the marked paths. Easier to avoid surprises that way."

Emma wasn't sure what he meant, but a small shiver traveled down her spine - half fear, half intrigue.

"Night, Emma," he said warmly. "Welcome to Saddle Creek."

She whispered a "goodnight" back as he headed inside.

Willow. The name echoed again through her thoughts. She hadn't planned on getting attached to anything here - not yet, maybe not ever—but something about that mare stirred an unexpected flutter of hope.

She returned inside when the porch light flickered. Her dad came in behind her, brushing dust off his jeans.

"Well!" he said cheerfully. "First night in the new house. Think we'll survive?"

Her mom smiled at Emma. "How about tomorrow we explore town? Maybe peek at the stables?"

Emma hesitated. She didn't want to seem too eager - didn't want her parents thinking she was adjusting too quickly or forgetting what she'd left behind. But the image of the chestnut mare lingered behind her eyelids, warm and insistent.

"Sure," she said softly. "Maybe."

Her parents exchanged a relieved look.

Later, after brushing her teeth and unpacking the essentials, Emma changed into pajamas and crawled into bed. The sheets were unfamiliar, the mattress firmer than her old one, and the shadows in the corners shifted differently in the moonlight. But she was too tired to care much.

Through the window, the forest stretched dark and silent. A small breeze rattled the leaves. Emma closed her eyes, letting the sounds of the new night wash over her.

She must have dozed off, because suddenly she was half-awake again, unsure how much time had passed. A faint sound drifted through the window - soft, distant, almost questioning. Not quite a whinny... not quite a cry.

Emma sat up. She held her breath, listening.

Nothing.

Just the whisper of wind.

She shook her head and lay back down. She was imagining things. Moving was stressful. New surroundings did strange things to your ears. She pulled the blanket up to her chin.

This time, when she closed her eyes, the image of Willow filled the darkness behind them - the chestnut mare standing alone in the pasture, watching her with bright, intelligent eyes.

Something fluttered in Emma's chest again. Curiosity. Connection. A feeling she hadn't expected to find on the first day.

Maybe - *maybe* - moving wouldn't be awful.

But she didn't dare think it fully. Not yet.

She rolled onto her side and let the steady rustling of leaves lull her back toward sleep.

Tomorrow, she told herself, she'd see the town. And maybe the stables.

And maybe - if she was lucky - she'd see Willow again.

Outside, the woods shifted in the moonlight, deep and quiet. And somewhere far off, barely within hearing range, a soft sound echoed through the trees.

A sound Emma didn't hear.

A sound like a lonely, frightened whinny.
One that would matter very soon.
But for tonight, Emma slept.
And Saddle Creek waited for morning.

Chapter Two

Emma woke to a pale strip of morning light stretched across her bedroom floor. For a moment she forgot where she was. The ceiling looked wrong. The air smelled different. Her sheets were not the ones she had slept under for years. She blinked slowly and remembered. Saddle Creek. The house on Pine Hollow Road. The new beginning she had not asked for.

She pushed herself upright and rubbed her eyes. The forest outside her window whispered with early birdsong. A cool breeze slipped in through the slightly open window and carried that same earthy scent she had noticed the night before. She could not decide if she liked it or not.

Her alarm clock read 7:14. Her parents were already awake. She could hear her mom humming in the kitchen. It sounded cheerful. Too cheerful for someone who had just spent a full day unpacking.

Emma dressed quickly and padded downstairs. Her mom stood over a skillet of eggs, spatula in hand, wearing a bright blue sweater that matched the kitchen tiles and her own mood. Her dad was on the porch fixing something on the old swing even though it was far too early to be working on anything.

"Good morning, sweetheart," her mom said. "Hungry?"

"Sort of," Emma said. She took a seat at the table. A carton of orange juice sat beside a pile of mail that had arrived early. The labels still read Hayes Family, Old Address. It felt strange to see them in this new space.

"You slept well, I hope," her mom added.

"Yeah. Mostly."

Her dad poked his head through the open door. "The hardware store opens at nine. I might pick up some tools. Want to come?"

Emma shrugged. "Maybe later."

Her mom fixed her with that knowing look that said she understood far more than she let on. "We thought we might take a walk around town after breakfast. Just to get familiar with things. And maybe stop by the stables. If that sounds good."

Emma hesitated. She wanted to see the mare again. She had not been able to stop thinking about her. But admitting she wanted to go felt like giving in to something. Like letting this place win her over.

"I guess looking is fine," she said carefully.

Her mom smiled. "Perfect."

Saddle Creek looked different in the daylight. The morning sun lit the rooftops with warm gold. Sparrows swooped between hedges. The air carried a subtle sweetness from the pine trees nearby. As they walked toward the town center, Emma noticed that everyone they passed seemed to know each other. People waved from porches. A woman unloading her car shouted a cheerful greeting to a jogger. A pair of boys on skateboards zipped past with friendly nods.

It was the kind of place where people probably remembered your name after meeting you once.

They passed The Giddy Up Grill. The mural in the sunlight was even more beautiful than it had been the previous day. Horses galloped through a painted meadow so vividly that Emma half expected the figures to leap off the wall.

"That was not here fifteen years ago," her dad said as they walked by. "Looks new. I like it."

Farther down the road, an antique shop sat between a bakery and a post office. Wooden horses hung in the bakery window, each one carved in a different pose. A sign on the post office door announced an upcoming charity fun ride. Everywhere she looked there were signs of horses, trails, saddles, and barns. It felt like the entire town revolved around the rhythm of hoofbeats.

By the time they reached the white fencing of Saddle Creek Stables, Emma felt a fluttering inside her chest that she had been trying very hard to ignore.

Her mom rested a hand on her shoulder. "Ready?"

Emma nodded.

The gate was open. A gravel path stretched toward a cluster of red roofed barns nestled against the base of Hillcrest Woods. The barns were arranged in a half circle that made the place look inviting rather than intimidating. Birds perched on the ridge lines, chirping cheerfully.

"Look at that view," her dad said softly.

Emma hardly heard him. She was scanning the pasture near the road, searching for the chestnut mare. The grass sparkled with dew. Several horses grazed lazily, flicking their tails at the occasional insect.

But not her.

The chestnut mare was nowhere in sight.

A little pang of disappointment tightened in Emma's stomach.

Her mom noticed. "Maybe she is in one of the paddocks closer to the barn."

They followed the gravel path. A sign near the entrance welcomed visitors and listed the stable rules. Emma read them out of habit even though her parents were already walking ahead. No running. No sudden noises. No feeding the horses. Helmet required for all riders.

Before she could finish, a cheerful voice called out. "Hi there. Can I help you folks?"

A woman in her fifties walked over from the nearest barn. She had sun kissed skin, a firm posture, and bright eyes that suggested she had been around horses for a long time. She wore a faded maroon stable jacket and tan breeches. A long braid hung down her back.

"Morning," Emma's mom said warmly. "We just moved into town yesterday. We thought we would come take a look."

The woman smiled. "Welcome to Saddle Creek. I am Marlene. I run the lesson program here."

Her handshake was confident and warm. Emma liked her instantly.

"This must be Emma," Marlene said. "You look like you are already curious about the place."

Emma tried not to blush. "A little."

Marlene laughed gently. "Curious is good. Horses need people with curious minds."

She gestured toward the barns. "Come on. I will give you a quick tour. We usually have riders on weekends, but it is quieter this morning."

Emma fell into step beside her parents as they followed Marlene toward the first barn. The gravel crunched under their shoes.

Inside, the barn was bright and airy. Sunlight streamed in through skylights overhead. Stalls lined both sides, each one clean and neat with a nameplate on the door. Some horses poked their heads out, sniffing the new arrivals. Others nibbled at their hay with contented sighs.

Emma felt something warm spread through her chest. She had missed the smell of horses. It had been years since she last visited a stable, and she had forgotten how grounding it felt. The mixture of hay, leather, and warm coats was strangely comforting.

Marlene stopped beside a gentle looking gray gelding named Pepper. He lifted his head and sniffed Emma's sleeve.

"This one is Pepper," Marlene said. "Kind as they come. Great with younger riders."

Pepper blinked his soft brown eyes at Emma. She smiled without realizing it.

"Do you offer beginner lessons?" her mom asked.

"Absolutely," Marlene replied. "We have group classes on Tuesdays and Saturdays, and private sessions during the week. And we always start with an assessment lesson so we can match each rider to the right horse."

Emma nodded quietly. Her heart raced a little. The idea of starting lessons again was thrilling, but also scary. What if she had forgotten everything she used to know.

"Is Willow in this barn?" a voice behind them asked suddenly.

Emma turned to see a boy about her age carrying a water bucket. He had messy blond hair and a wide grin that made it impossible to tell if he was about to crack a joke or had just finished one. He balanced the bucket with one hand like it weighed nothing.

"Jake," Marlene said with a patient smile. "You are supposed to be mucking the west stalls."

"I am," Jake said. He shifted the bucket to his other hand. "I just, you know, got curious. People usually ask about Willow first."

Emma blinked. "Willow is the chestnut mare, right?"

Jake brightened. "Yep. The one with the attitude and the beauty queen face."

Emma's heartbeat quickened. "Where is she?"

"In the big paddock behind the training arena," Jake replied. "She likes the morning sun."

Marlene gave the boy a look that managed to be both teasing and disciplinary at once. "You can introduce our new guests when your chores are finished."

Jake gave a dramatic sigh. "Fine. But someone needs to warn them that Willow has opinions." He winked at Emma. "Good luck."

He disappeared around the corner with the water bucket sloshing beside him.

Emma felt her curiosity growing stronger by the second.

Marlene led her parents toward the tack room, but Emma found herself drifting slightly behind. Her gaze kept slipping toward the path that led around the side of the barn. She could see a flash of fencing, a circle of sand that must be the training arena, and the tops of a few trees swaying in the breeze.

Her mom glanced over her shoulder and smiled. "We will go see her in a moment."

Emma blushed and nodded.

The tack room smelled of leather and polish. Saddles hung on wall racks. Bridles dangled neatly from hooks, each one oiled and cared for. A shelf of grooming brushes gleamed with fresh bristles.

"Riding takes a lot of responsibility," Marlene explained as Emma and her parents looked around. "We teach more than riding here. We teach horsemanship, care, safety, and respect. The horses are partners, not equipment."

Emma nodded. She liked the way Marlene talked about horses. It felt genuine.

After the tack room, they stepped back outside. The sun was climbing higher now. The air warmed slightly. A few riders arrived, helmets in hand, chatting excitedly.

"Would you like to see Willow?" Marlene asked with a sly smile, as if she already knew the answer.

"Yes," Emma said before she could hide the eagerness in her voice.

Her parents exchanged a pleased glance.

Marlene led them along the path behind the barn. The training arena stretched out to their right, bordered by tall oaks. Beyond that lay a large paddock with a wide wooden shelter and a trough near the fence.

Emma scanned the field with her breath caught in her throat.

Then she saw her.

Willow stood near the far corner, head low as she grazed. Her chestnut coat shimmered in the morning sun. A white blaze ran down her face, straight and delicate. Her tail swished lazily. She radiated strength, grace, and something else that Emma could not name.

Her heart lifted in an unexpected surge.

"She is beautiful," Emma whispered.

Marlene nodded. "She truly is. Willow is one of our most talented horses. But she is sensitive. She needs a confident rider who understands her moods."

Jake reappeared at the fence, leaning casually on the top rail. "And she likes to pretend she is the queen of the barn."

"Jake," Marlene said. "The stalls."

"I am going," he replied with a grin. "But first, watch this."

He puckered his lips and made a little clicking sound. Willow lifted her head sharply. She turned toward them, ears pricked. For a moment she stood absolutely still, watching Jake with focused intensity.

Then she began to walk toward the fence.

Emma felt her breath catch. The mare's movement was smooth and deliberate. Her muscles rippled beneath her coat with every step. Her mane fluttered in the breeze.

She reached the fence with a soft snort and fixed her gaze on Jake.

"See," Jake said proudly. "She likes me."

Willow pushed her nose toward his jacket pocket.

Jake laughed. "No treats today. Sorry, girl."

She huffed impatiently and swiveled her ears toward Emma.

Emma froze.

The mare blinked slowly, studying her with deep, intelligent eyes. The same eyes that had found her from the roadside yesterday. Something warmed inside Emma. Recognition. Connection. A spark she had never felt in her old town.

"She likes you," Jake said with surprise.

Marlene raised an eyebrow. "Willow does not usually approach new people on the first meeting."

Emma stepped closer to the fence, unsure if she was doing the right thing. Willow lowered her head. Emma reached out gently.

The mare sniffed her palm, then nudged it softly with her velvety muzzle. A warm breath brushed across Emma's skin. Emma felt her heart melt.

"Wow," Jake whispered.

Her parents watched with surprise and delight.

Marlene folded her arms, thoughtful. "Interesting."

Emma scratched Willow lightly between the eyes. The mare leaned into it. Her ears relaxed. Her whole posture softened.

"She really does like you," Marlene said. "That is rare."

Emma felt a swell of something proud and fragile. "Do lots of people work with her?"

"Not many," Marlene said. "She has a strong personality. Some riders find her too challenging. She needs patience. And understanding."

Willow nudged Emma's shoulder gently as if agreeing.

Emma's smile widened. She felt something shift inside her. A tiny piece of her that had been tight and closed since the move suddenly cracked open. Air rushed in. Hope crept through.

"Would you like to meet some of our other horses?" Marlene asked.

"Can we come back to Willow later?" Emma asked quietly.

"Of course."

Jake laughed. "Willow already claimed you. She is like that."

Emma chuckled, even though she was not sure he was joking.

After the tour, they stopped at the small stable office to pick up a lesson brochure. While her parents chatted with Marlene about scheduling and safety forms, Emma stepped outside for a moment.

Willow was still in the paddock, grazing peacefully. A gust of wind swept across the field, rustling the leaves behind her. Willow lifted her head suddenly, ears pinned toward the forest. Her entire body stiffened.

Emma frowned.

Another gust of wind followed. Then a very faint sound drifted from the tree line. A rustle. Or a cry. Or something in between.

Willow snorted and stamped her hoof.

Jake approached Emma from the side. "She has been jumpy the past few days."

"Why?" Emma asked.

Jake scrunched up one shoulder. "Could be anything. Coyotes. A loose dog. Weird noises from the woods. Animals get spooked easily."

Emma listened harder. The woods were quiet now. Completely calm.

"Does that happen a lot?" she asked.

Jake leaned on the fence. "Sometimes. Especially near Crestwood Trail. That place is strange lately."

Emma swallowed. "Strange how?"

Jake opened his mouth to answer, but Marlene called him sharply. "Jake. Stalls."

He sighed and trotted away.

Emma stood alone for a moment, staring into the edge of the woods. The trees swayed gently. Shadows shifted like living things.

Something about that forest made her skin prickle.

Willow flicked her tail and went back to grazing.

Emma exhaled and walked back to her parents.

On the walk home, her mom squeezed her arm with a gentle smile. "Well. What do you think?"

Emma did not want to sound too excited. But she could not hide the spark in her voice. "It was really nice."

Her dad laughed. "Nice is a big compliment from you right now."

Emma shrugged, embarrassed.

"You connected with Willow," her mom said. "I saw it."

Emma looked down at her shoes. "Maybe."

Her father ruffled her hair. "I think you did."

She did not argue.

When they reached the house, Emma went upstairs to her room. She dropped onto her bed and stared up at the slanted ceiling. She felt tired, but in a good way. The kind of tired that came from being outside and breathing fresh air and touching velvet soft horse noses.

She closed her eyes.

Willow appeared instantly in her mind. The chestnut coat. The warm eyes. The soft nudge. The way the mare had looked straight at her as if they already knew each other.

A tiny smile crept across Emma's lips.

Maybe moving had not been the end of the world.

Maybe it was the start of something she could not quite imagine yet.

She rolled onto her side and looked out the window. The forest loomed beyond the yard, quiet and dark. Somewhere deep inside those trees, something waited for its moment.

Emma did not know it yet.

But Willow did.

And soon, Emma would too.

For now, the new life of Saddle Creek was unfolding gently. Slowly. Steadily.

And Emma Hayes was already part of it.

Chapter Three

Emma woke the next morning with a buzzing in her stomach that felt like a swarm of nervous butterflies. It took her a moment to understand why. Then she remembered. Today was her first lesson at Saddle Creek Stables.

She stared up at the slanted ceiling while a slow smile tugged at her mouth. She tried to smother it, but it slipped out anyway. Even with the mixture of excitement and fear, something bright pulsed beneath everything. She was going back to see Willow. And she was going to ride again for the first time in years.

Her alarm clock glowed 7:02.

She rolled out of bed and padded to the window. The early morning light filtered through the trees, giving the whole forest a soft, misty glow. A few birds hopped along the branches. One sang a long, clear note that rose into the sky like a ribbon. Emma felt her nerves tug tighter.

She dressed slowly. Riding pants she had not worn since she was ten. A fitted T shirt. A jacket tied around her waist. She brushed her hair and tied it back. Her reflection in the mirror looked like a girl who was trying very hard to be calm. The flutter in her stomach disagreed.

Downstairs, the house was already filled with the smell of pancakes. Her father flipped a new batch while her mother placed fresh fruit on the table.

Her mom noticed her outfit right away. "You look ready."

Emma shrugged, pretending her heart was not pounding like a drum. "I guess."

Her dad smiled in that soft way he saved for moments he knew were important. "We will take the car. Give us ten minutes."

Emma sat at the table and pushed a few blueberries around with her fork before forcing herself to eat. Her stomach felt too light, but she knew she needed something.

Her mom poured her orange juice. "You are going to have a great time."

Emma wished she could believe it as easily as her mom said it.

The drive to the stables was short, but Emma felt every bump in the road. Pine trees arched overhead as they approached the familiar white fences. When the red roofed barns came into view, her pulse quickened. Horses grazed in the morning sun, their coats glowing like polished stone.

Somewhere behind those fences, Willow was waking up too.

The thought steadied her a little.

Her dad parked near the stable entrance. "Want us to walk you in?"

Emma shook her head. "I can go by myself. I am not five."

Her mom smiled. "Fair enough. But we will stay nearby in case you need us."

Emma stepped out of the car and inhaled deeply. The air smelled like dew soaked grass, hay, and the faintest hint of warm earth. It was a smell that felt like childhood, like hope, like something just beginning.

She followed the gravel path toward the main barn. A few riders were already there with helmets tucked under their arms. Others led horses toward the arena. Hoofbeats echoed faintly across the yard, rhythmic and steady.

Inside the barn, the air was warmer. Horses poked their heads out of their stalls. A chestnut gelding snorted softly as Emma passed. A bay mare flicked an ear, watching her with calm curiosity.

Emma reached the viewing benches near the arena door and sat. Her palms were already sweaty. Her heart thumped against her ribs.

She did not want to mess up. Not in front of strangers. Not in front of Willow, even though she was not riding her today. And definitely not in front of Riley, who she suspected would find any mistake hilarious.

She swallowed hard.

Footsteps approached.

"Hey, new girl."

Emma looked up just in time to see Jake drop onto the seat beside her. His hair stuck out in five different directions, and he carried a helmet decorated with stickers of cartoon goats doing karate. She stared at it, unsure if it was supposed to be funny or if Jake simply lived on a different wavelength from the rest of humanity.

"Nervous?" he asked with a grin.

"A little," Emma admitted.

"Good. Shows you care. People who are never nervous are usually the ones who end up falling into the water trough. And trust me, that is not a fun place to be."

Emma laughed before she could stop herself. The sound came out shaky, but it helped.

Jake nudged her shoulder lightly. "You will do great. Marlene is amazing."

"Are you riding today?" Emma asked.

"Nope. Lessons for me are on Thursdays. But I am here for chores. I finished the early ones, so I can hang out for a bit and judge your skills."

Emma's eyebrows rose in alarm.

"I am kidding," Jake said quickly. "Mostly."

Before she could respond, a familiar voice cut through the aisle.

"Oh. It is you."

Riley stood near the chalkboard where the lesson schedule was posted. Her black riding jacket looked like it had been polished. Her helmet gleamed. Even her ponytail was intimidating.

Jake muttered under his breath, "Perfect timing, Riley."

Riley ignored him. Her gaze pinned Emma like a butterfly to a cork board. "So you are taking a lesson? On what horse?"

Emma swallowed, wishing she had the answer written on her forehead.

Marlene appeared from the tack room at that moment. "Good morning, everyone. Emma, I would like you to meet me in the grooming area. You will be riding Maple today."

Riley smirked. "Maple is easy. Like, really easy. A baby could handle him."

Jake crossed his arms. "Not everyone has to start on a dragon like Stormwatch."

Riley tossed her hair and marched away.

Emma felt her cheeks burn.

Jake sighed. "She is not that bad. Well, she sort of is. But you get used to her. Come on. Maple is nice. You will like him."

They walked together to the grooming stalls. Maple stood quietly in the first one, tied with cross ties, his bay coat shining. He was smaller than Willow and had a sweet, gentle face with soft brown eyes that reminded Emma of a stuffed animal she had when she was little.

"This is Maple," Marlene said warmly. "He is steady and patient, which makes him perfect for your assessment lesson."

Emma moved closer and offered her hand. Maple sniffed it politely, then nudged her arm as if asking whether she had brought snacks.

Emma smiled. "Hi, Maple."

"He likes you," Marlene said. "Grab a brush from the table and give him a good curry. Gentle circles. Firm pressure."

Emma picked up the soft curry comb and began brushing Maple's shoulder. At first her movements were stiff. But as she felt the rhythm of the strokes and Maple's relaxed breathing, she loosened up. Soon she found herself brushing with calm, steady motions.

"Great job," Marlene said. "Now use the hard brush to flick away the dirt."

Emma did, following every instruction. Jake hovered nearby offering commentary that was sometimes helpful and sometimes questionable.

"Remember to brush his belly. But not too close to the back legs. Unless you want a hoof shaped bruise."

"Do not forget the withers. Maple loves those."

"If he yawns while you groom his ears, it means he thinks he is at a spa."

Emma laughed again, more easily this time.

When Maple was fully groomed, Marlene showed her how to place the saddle pad, then lift the saddle. It was heavier than Emma remembered. She almost lost her grip, but managed to settle it gently onto Maple's back.

"Nice work," Marlene said. "Now the girth."

Emma tightened it slowly. Maple puffed out his belly in rebellion.

Jake snorted. "Classic Maple. He always tries that."

Emma pulled the girth a little tighter. This time it stayed.

After the bridle was on, they walked Maple to the training arena. The sand felt soft under Emma's boots. The sun shone brightly overhead, warming her back. The arena rails cast long shadows across the footing.

Riley leaned on the far fence, pretending not to watch. Emma tried to ignore her.

Marlene set the mounting block near Maple's side.

Emma's stomach twisted.

She remembered falling once during a pony ride years ago. It had not been serious. She had barely scraped her knee. But the memory had lingered in the back of her mind like a stubborn weed.

She swallowed hard.

"You can do it," Jake said quietly.

Emma stepped onto the block. Maple stood steady, patient as ever. She gathered the reins, placed her left foot in the stirrup, and swung her leg over. Her balance wobbled for a second, but she settled into the saddle with a deep breath.

"You look good up there," Marlene said. "Take a moment to sit tall. Shoulders back. Eyes up."

Emma straightened slowly. The saddle felt firm but supportive. Maple's warmth rose through her legs.

She felt safe.

Marlene stepped to the center of the arena. "All right. Walk on."

Emma squeezed gently. Maple stepped forward with a calm, even stride. Emma felt the familiar rock of his movement and her nerves melted slightly.

"Good," Marlene said. "Follow the rail. Keep an eye on where you are going."

Emma guided Maple along the outer edge of the arena. The reins felt strange in her hands at first, but gradually she found a rhythm. Maple's ears flicked forward, relaxed, listening.

"Your posture looks great," Marlene called. "Let your hips follow his movement."

Emma adjusted, letting her body sway with Maple. A small hum of confidence rose in her chest.

She glanced toward the fence. Riley crossed her arms, watching intently. Emma could not tell if she was judging or sizing her up. She looked away quickly, not wanting to lose focus.

After ten minutes of walking, Marlene asked her to halt. Maple stopped with a gentle shift of weight.

"Nice," Marlene said. "Let us try a little steering. Bring him onto a large circle."

Emma guided Maple away from the rail. The circle she created was a little egg shaped at first, but Marlene offered gentle corrections.

"Use your inside leg to encourage him to bend. Think of leading him with the inside rein while the outside rein supports the shape."

Emma tried again. This time the circle came out rounder.

Jake pumped a fist in the air from his seat on a hay bale. "Yes, new girl. That was great."

Emma smiled even as her face warmed.

After more circles, serpentines, and transitions, Emma felt a calm settle over her. Maple was steady and reliable. Riding him felt like walking with an old friend who always matched your pace.

"All right," Marlene said after a while. "Let us try a little trot."

Emma's heart leaped again. She nodded.

Marlene instructed, "Ask him with a light squeeze. Sit tall. Do not lean forward. Trust him."

Emma took a deep breath. She squeezed gently.

Maple lifted into a trot.

Emma jolted once, then twice. The trot felt bouncy, all rhythm and movement. She tried to post, rising and sitting with the movement, but her timing was off.

Her legs wobbled. Her balance slipped. For a moment she panicked.

But Maple kept going at a steady pace, patient and calm.

"You have it," Marlene encouraged. "Rise when his outside shoulder comes forward. Look ahead. Not down."

Emma fixed her gaze on the far fence. Rise. Sit. Rise. Sit. Eventually she found a moment where her body matched Maple's rhythm. The motion clicked.

A thrill raced up her spine.

She was doing it.

She was riding again.

When they slowed back to a walk, Emma felt breathless but proud.

Jake cupped his hands around his mouth. "That was actually really good."

Riley pushed off the fence. "Not bad for a beginner."

Emma stiffened, unsure if it was a compliment or an insult.

Riley added, "At least you did not fall off."

Emma's cheeks turned pink, but Marlene's voice cut in. "Riley, why do you not go saddle up Stormwatch if you are going to hover here with commentary."

Riley rolled her eyes and walked away, though Emma noticed she did not look quite as smug as before.

The rest of the lesson passed smoothly. Emma practiced more walking and trotting, more steering, more circles. Maple stayed kind and steady.

When the lesson finally ended, Emma slid off Maple and landed lightly on the ground. Her legs wobbled but she caught herself.

Marlene patted her shoulder. "Well done. You have natural balance and a good feel for the reins. Maple responded beautifully. I think you are ready for regular lessons."

Emma's eyes brightened. "Really?"

"Absolutely."

Jake nodded eagerly. "Told you."

They untacked Maple together. Emma brushed his coat once more, feeling a stronger connection now that they had worked as a team. Maple leaned gently into the brush, clearly enjoying the attention.

"Good boy," Emma whispered softly.

After Maple was returned to his stall, Emma stepped out of the barn for some fresh air. The sun had risen higher and the forest shimmered in the warmth.

Then she felt something.

A gaze.

She turned toward the far paddock.

Willow stood beside the fence, her ears pointed forward, watching Emma with an unreadable expression. Calm. Curious. Assessing.

Emma took a step toward her, almost without realizing it. Willow blinked slowly and shifted her weight. Her mane fluttered in the breeze like a flame.

Emma smiled.

She did not call out. She did not wave. She simply stood there, letting the quiet connection settle between them.

The world felt still for a moment.

Then Willow lowered her head and returned to grazing.

Emma exhaled, light and steady.

She started walking back to her parents, who were waiting by the car.

"How was it?" her mom asked.

A grin spread across Emma's face, warm and real. "It was amazing."

Her dad handed her a bottle of water. "We watched some of it from the viewing area. You looked like you belonged up there."

Emma felt her chest fill with pride. "I liked Maple a lot."

Her mom glanced toward the paddock. "And Willow watched you for a long time."

Emma felt her cheeks warm. "Maybe."

The three of them walked toward the parking lot.

As they reached the car, Emma looked back one more time at the barns, the arena, and the quiet paddock where Willow grazed. Another gentle flutter stirred in her chest.

She could feel something beginning. Something new and important. Something she had not expected when she arrived in Saddle Creek.

Riding was coming back to her. Slowly. Steadily.

And Willow had noticed her.

Whatever happened next, Emma knew this was the start of something big.

She could feel it in her heartbeat.

She could feel it in the saddle soreness already settling into her legs.

She could feel it in the quiet, unwavering way Willow had watched her.

This place was becoming part of her story.

And she was becoming part of Saddle Creek.

Chapter Four

Emma arrived at Saddle Creek Stables the following Saturday with a tight mix of anticipation and uneasiness coiled in her stomach. The sky overhead was a soft blue, brushed with streaks of pink that still lingered from sunrise. The early air carried a coolness that made her inhale deeper than usual, almost as if her lungs were trying to gather courage.

She held her riding helmet against her side as she walked along the gravel path toward the main barn. Maple's lesson earlier in the week had given her confidence, but that confidence seemed determined to hide this morning. Today felt different. Today she was not just learning. Today she was stepping into the rhythms of the barn on a busy weekend when everyone else seemed to already know exactly how things worked.

Her mom waved from the car before driving off. "Text me if you need anything. Have fun."

Emma nodded and tried to smile, but her stomach felt like it had filled with small stones.

Inside the barn, everything hummed with activity. Riders tightened girths, grabbed grooming kits, chatted, filled buckets, and led horses to the arena. Hooves clacked gently against the concrete. Horses swished tails or nickered softly as people passed.

Emma paused near the entrance to gather her thoughts, only to hear a familiar voice behind her.

"Well, look who is back."

She turned to see Riley standing with her arms crossed and one hip shifted slightly, like she had been waiting there on purpose. Her riding boots gleamed, and her dark hair was tied in a flawless ponytail. Even her gloves looked intimidating.

"Hi, Riley," Emma said, doing her best to keep her voice steady.

Riley raised an eyebrow. "So. Maple was not too hard for you?"

"No," Emma replied. "He was great."

"Maple is always great." Riley's tone sharpened a little. "Which is why beginners get him."

Emma forced herself not to shrink.

Jake appeared suddenly from the tack room carrying two lead ropes and wearing an expression of mild panic. "Riley. Marlene needs you to help tie hay nets. She said now. Not later."

Riley stared at him for a moment, trying to decide whether she believed him. Jake widened his eyes dramatically and gave the slightest nod toward the office door. A beat later, Marlene's voice called for assistance.

Riley sighed and tossed her ponytail. "Fine. But I am watching you, new girl."

Emma held very still as Riley strode toward the hay shed. Only when she disappeared did Emma breathe again.

Jake grinned. "You are welcome."

Emma exhaled softly. "Thanks."

"She is not always like this," Jake said with a shrug. "Well. Actually, she sort of is. But she gets better once she stops deciding you are a threat."

"A threat?" Emma blinked. "I have been here for less than a week."

Jake laughed. "Exactly."

Before Emma could ask what he meant, Marlene walked in from the far end of the barn, clipboard in hand.

"Good morning, Emma. Glad you could make it again." Marlene smiled warmly. "You will be working with Maple today, but I want to show you more of the barn first. Chores are part of becoming a real rider."

Emma nodded. "Sure."

Jake pumped a fist. "You are officially joining the workforce."

Marlene pretended not to hear him. "Let us start with learning how to muck a stall."

Emma tried to hide her fascination as Marlene handed her a pitchfork. She had never mucked a stall before, and the idea made her feel strangely official. Almost like a real horse person.

They entered Pepper's stall first. The gelding lifted his head and sniffed Emma's sleeve.

"Begin by picking out the wet patches and manure balls," Marlene explained. "Shake the clean shavings free by gently tapping the fork."

Emma nodded and got to work. At first she moved slowly, uncertain about where to stand or how close she could get to Pepper's hooves. Marlene guided her with calm instructions, adjusting her stance and showing her how to scoop and sift the bedding. Soon Emma found a rhythm.

Pepper watched her with sleepy interest.

"You are doing great," Marlene said. "Try not to overfill the fork. A lighter load is easier to control."

Emma followed the advice. She noticed Pepper was perfectly content with her presence. That alone made her shoulders loosen.

"You can do the next stall on your own," Marlene said. "It belongs to Maple."

Emma smiled, feeling a mix of pride and nerves. She crossed the aisle and entered Maple's stall. Maple was already in the cross ties being groomed by a younger girl, so the space was empty. The smell of hay mixed with the earthy scent of shavings.

Emma began working. Scoop. Shake. Push. Lift. Her movements were slow at first, but they grew more confident.

She was nearly done when she heard footsteps stop behind her.

"That is not how you do it."

Emma froze.

Riley leaned against Maple's stall door, arms still crossed. Her expression looked like she was watching a documentary about someone doing everything wrong.

Emma held the pitchfork a little tighter. "Marlene said this was correct."

Riley scoffed softly. "It is fine. But not good." She stepped inside, picked up a second fork, and began demonstrating with sharp, practiced motions. "You have to angle it this way or you will miss half the mess. See?"

Emma watched carefully, adjusting her grip.

"Try again," Riley said.

Emma took the pitchfork and attempted the angle Riley showed her. The fork sank neatly under a patch of soiled shavings. She lifted it and shook gently.

Riley stepped back. "Better."

Emma blinked. "Oh. Thanks."

Riley looked thrown off for a second, as if she had been expecting Emma to fight her or freeze entirely. She cleared her throat. "Just do not let Maple stand in dirty bedding. He gets hock sores easily. And Marlene will blame me."

Emma frowned. "Why would she blame you?"

"Because I am Maple's assigned rider when he is not in lessons," Riley said. "Or I was. Before Stormwatch."

Emma hesitated. "Do you not like Stormwatch?"

Riley paused for a moment. Her expression softened just slightly, revealing something like frustration mixed with longing. "Stormwatch is amazing. But he is not easy. And sometimes I miss Maple."

Before Emma could respond, Jake skidded into the aisle, nearly dropping a stack of empty buckets.

"Riley. Marlene wants you to help set up jumps."

Riley stiffened. "Now?"

"Yes. Emergency. The poles are attacking."

"They do not attack."

"Today they do."

Riley groaned and marched off.

Jake leaned into the stall doorway. "You survived the Riley test. Level one complete."

Emma laughed under her breath. "She was not that bad this time."

"She is trying to figure you out," Jake said. "Also she likes teaching people things. But she does not like admitting she likes it."

Emma smiled. "That checks out."

After chores, Emma met Maple in the grooming area. His coat gleamed under the light as he shifted calmly in the cross ties.

Emma began brushing him, and Maple sighed happily as she worked along his back.

"You two get along well," Marlene observed as she approached with a smile.

Emma felt warmth spread through her. "He is really sweet."

"And he trusts you. That is important."

Emma's heart fluttered. Trust was a big word. A word she did not hear often from people. Hearing it from a horse felt even more meaningful.

They finished grooming Maple and tacked him up. When they walked to the arena, Emma's pulse quickened again. Today was her second time riding, and she wanted to show improvement.

She mounted with a steadier swing of her leg this time. Maple stepped forward with confident, even strides. Emma followed his motion, shoulders relaxed.

Marlene guided her through exercises that felt familiar, but this time Emma felt more grounded. They practiced walk to trot transitions, larger circles, steering patterns, and a slightly faster trot. Maple responded with calm willingness.

"You are doing beautifully," Marlene called from the center of the arena. "Your posture is excellent."

Emma felt pride bloom in her chest.

She trotted around the far end of the arena, focusing on rhythm, when she heard someone shout from outside the fence.

"Emma, your diagonal!"

She glanced toward the voice and saw Riley leaning on the rail.

Emma's face grew hot. She looked down at Maple's shoulder, then back up, adjusting her rise.

Riley gave a tiny nod, almost approving.

Marlene turned. "Riley, are you coaching or riding?"

Riley flushed and stepped back. "Riding. I am riding."

Jake laughed from the bleachers. "Caught."

The moment passed, and Emma returned to riding. After a long session, Maple slowed to a walk as Emma cooled him down. Her legs felt pleasantly tired. Her heart felt light.

When she dismounted, Marlene gave her an encouraging smile. "You have natural talent, Emma. I want you to know that."

Emma's cheeks warmed. "Thank you."

"You are gentle but confident. Horses respond well to that."

Emma looked toward the paddock where Willow grazed. The chestnut mare lifted her head as if sensing the attention.

Something stirred inside Emma again. A quiet, hopeful warmth.

After her lesson, Emma returned to the barn to help untack Maple. She placed his saddle on its stand and carefully wiped down his bridle. She brushed Maple's coat until it shone.

Then Marlene called her over. "Emma, before you leave, would you like to help me bring Willow in from the paddock?"

Emma froze.

"Me?" she asked softly.

"Yes. She already seems interested in you. And I want you to learn how to handle different horses."

Emma nodded too fast. "Yes. I would really like to."

Jake popped his head over a hay bale. "Good luck. She is in queen mode today."

Emma's hands felt sweaty, but she followed Marlene out to the paddock.

Willow stood near the far fence, grazing with her tail flicking lazily. Her coat gleamed in the sunlight, deep chestnut with golden highlights. She lifted her head as Emma and Marlene approached.

Her ears pricked forward. She did not step back.

"She remembers you," Marlene said.

Emma's heart thudded in her chest.

Marlene opened the gate. "Walk slowly. Speak softly. Offer your hand."

Emma stepped forward, her breath shallow. Willow watched every movement.

"Hi, Willow," Emma whispered.

The mare blinked and stepped closer. Her warm breath brushed across Emma's palm. Emma gently clipped the lead rope to her halter. Willow accepted it without hesitation.

"You are doing great," Marlene said quietly.

Emma led Willow out of the paddock. The mare walked beside her with a smooth, powerful stride, her ears relaxed. Emma felt the tension in her body ease with every step.

Then everything changed.

A loud bang echoed from the back of the barn. It sounded like a metal bucket slamming against concrete.

Willow froze. Her ears shot forward. Her muscles tensed like coiled springs.

Emma had no time to react.

Willow jumped sideways with a sharp snort.

Emma stumbled, almost losing her grip. Her heart lurched as Willow surged forward, her lead rope pulling taut.

Marlene moved instantly. "Emma, let go if you need to. I have her."

But Emma held on with both hands, feet digging into the earth. She was terrified, but something inside her refused to let go.

"Easy, Willow," she whispered, voice trembling.

Willow pranced in place, nostrils flared. For a few long seconds, Emma felt as if the ground had dropped out from under her.

Then Willow's eyes flicked toward Emma's voice. Her breathing slowed. Her feet stilled.

Emma kept whispering. "It is okay. You are okay."

Willow's muscles slowly relaxed. She lowered her head and exhaled.

Marlene stepped beside them with careful calm. "Very good, Emma. You handled that beautifully."

Emma felt her fingers shaking around the rope. "What was that noise?"

Jake jogged around the corner, panting. "Sorry. A bucket slipped off the hook. Totally my fault."

Riley emerged behind him, rolling her eyes. "Of course it was."

Jake threw up his hands. "Well, at least Willow did not run me over."

Marlene looked at Emma with soft pride. "You kept your composure. That was impressive."

Emma did not feel impressive. She felt shaky and surprised. But also strangely strong. Willow pressed her muzzle into Emma's arm as if apologizing.

Emma gently stroked her neck.

Riley stood with her hands on her hips. "Most people let go when Willow spooks." Then her expression shifted ever so slightly. "Not bad."

Emma blinked at her. Riley quickly looked away.

· · ·

After Willow was safely in her stall, Emma wiped the sweat from her palms and leaned against the wall with a long breath.

Jake approached with a guilty smile. "Sorry about the whole bucket fiasco. I swear it jumped."

Emma laughed shakily. "It is okay. Willow is just really sensitive."

"She is," Jake agreed. "She listens with her whole body. That mare sees everything."

Emma nodded. "She calmed down fast, though."

"Yes," Marlene said behind them. "Because she trusts you already."

Emma felt her heart lift. "Really?"

"Really."

Riley walked past at that moment, carrying a saddle. She glanced at Emma then at Willow. Something unreadable flickered across her face.

"She never trusted me that fast," Riley muttered under her breath.

Emma did not know whether she was meant to hear it.

She did.

And it left a small ache inside her.

When Emma finally left the barn, her legs still felt shaky from the scare. But her heart felt full. Her mom picked her up, and Emma spent the ride home replaying the scene in her mind.

Willow had spooked. Emma had stayed with her.

Willow had calmed because of her.

She could not explain why it mattered so much, but it did.

It mattered a lot.

Later that evening, Emma stood at her bedroom window. The forest behind the house swayed gently. Moonlight glimmered through the branches. Somewhere in the distance, an unfamiliar sound drifted through the dark. Not quite a whinny. Not quite a cry.

Emma leaned closer.

The sound faded.

She rubbed her arms and stepped away from the window.

Her thoughts drifted to Willow, and to the strange way the mare had tensed when the noise came earlier in the paddock. It reminded Emma of something Jake had said.

Sometimes the woods make strange noises.

Sometimes the horses notice things people do not.

Emma shivered again.

Still, when she finally slipped beneath her blankets and closed her eyes, the last thing she saw was Willow standing beside her, calm and steady despite the fright.

And that thought carried her gently into sleep.

Chapter Five

The next morning arrived with a soft drizzle that made the world look like it had been wrapped in a thin veil of silver threads. Raindrops tapped lightly against Emma's window, slipping down the glass in slow trails that shimmered in the faint light. The forest at the edge of the backyard looked misty and mysterious, as if the trees were whispering secrets she could almost hear.

Emma pulled on a warm sweater and watched the rain for a moment longer. Normally she would have groaned at a gloomy sky, but today she felt strangely calm. Almost eager. She was going back to the barn, and Marlene had said she could help with Willow's grooming.

Her stomach fluttered, but in a soft way. She tried not to smile too widely as she grabbed her riding boots and headed downstairs.

Her mother sat at the kitchen table with a cup of tea and a stack of work papers. She looked up when Emma entered.

"Morning, sweetheart. Looks like a wet day."

"Are you still taking me to the barn?" Emma asked as casually as she could.

Her mom smiled knowingly. "Of course. Rain does not stop horses or horse people."

Emma poured herself cereal and sat across from her. "Do you think the rain will make Willow extra jumpy?"

"Maybe. Maybe not." Her mom took a slow sip of tea. "You seem to handle her well. Trust yourself."

Emma stirred her cereal. "It did feel like she listened to me yesterday."

Her mom's smile softened. "I think she did."

The thought warmed Emma more than the sweater she wore. After breakfast, she gathered her bag and waited by the door.

The drive to the stables was quiet except for the gentle patter of rain against the roof of the car. Everything outside looked calm. The white fences gleamed faintly through the mist. Horses in the turnout paddocks wore rain sheets and grazed peacefully.

Emma stepped out of the car and inhaled the fresh smell of wet earth and pine. Her mom waved before driving off, and Emma tucked her hood up and jogged toward the barn.

Inside, the barn felt cozy and warm. The scent of hay and horses mixed with the earthy smell drifting in from the rain. A few riders brushed their horses or swept the aisle. Someone hummed near the tack room. The soft, steady rhythm of hooves shifting in stalls made the space feel alive.

Jake appeared from behind a stack of feed bags, holding a broom like a sword. "Ah. The new girl returns."

Emma laughed. "Morning, Jake."

He bowed dramatically. "The barn is chaotic today. Half the riders canceled, and the other half cannot decide if they should wear rain jackets or sweaters. Absolute disaster."

"You seem to be coping," Emma said.

"I am very brave," he replied. "Anyway, Marlene said you should go to Willow's stall. And she also said, and I quote, tell Emma to take her time and use calm energy. I do not know what that means, but horses probably do."

Emma's smile widened. "Thanks."

She walked down the aisle, past Maple and Pepper and Stormwatch. She paused briefly to scratch Pepper's forehead when he stretched his neck toward her. His breath warmed her hand.

Then she reached Willow's stall.

The chestnut mare stood with her head lowered, munching on flakes of hay. Her coat looked richer than ever in the dim morning light, the deep reddish brown almost glowing. She flicked an ear toward Emma without lifting her head.

Emma stepped closer. "Hi, Willow."

Willow lifted her head at the sound of her voice. Her large, dark eyes studied Emma with a calm interest. The memory of the previous day's scare flickered in Emma's mind, but Willow showed no sign of the tension she had displayed then.

Emma opened the stall door slowly and slipped inside, careful to latch it behind her. She approached Willow with a soft, steady breath.

Willow sniffed her jacket. Emma reached out and gently stroked the mare's neck.

"I missed you," she whispered before she could stop herself.

Willow exhaled a soft breath and leaned into the touch.

Emma felt something in her chest loosen, like a knot slowly unwinding.

Marlene approached quietly from the aisle. "Looks like she is glad to see you."

Emma turned. "Hi. Sorry. I did not see you."

"No need to apologize." Marlene leaned on the stall door with a gentle expression. "I wanted to see how she reacted to you this morning. You two are off to a very promising start."

Emma felt her face warm. "She is amazing."

"She can be," Marlene said. "But she also needs stability and trust from her handlers. She has had a few riders who tried to push her too quickly. She does not respond well to that."

Emma stroked Willow's shoulder thoughtfully. "She seems really sensitive."

"She is," Marlene agreed. "Sensitive horses are often the smartest ones. They notice everything, and they feel deeply. Willow needs someone who listens to her. Someone patient."

Emma's heart beat faster as she kept brushing Willow's neck. "I can do that."

"I know you can," Marlene said. "Which is why I want you to groom her today. Take your time. Let her tell you how she feels."

Emma nodded with quiet determination.

Marlene handed her a grooming kit. "Start with the soft brush today. Since the weather is damp, she does not need the curry comb everywhere."

Emma thanked her, and Marlene walked back down the aisle to talk to another rider.

Emma let out a slow breath and stepped closer to Willow. She picked up the soft brush and began in long, gentle strokes along Willow's shoulder.

Willow closed her eyes slightly.

Emma smiled. "That feels good, does it?"

The mare flicked an ear and shifted a little to let Emma reach a new spot.

Emma brushed her carefully from shoulder to flank. Willow's coat felt warm beneath the brush, and Emma felt calm settling over her, smoothing every frayed edge of her nerves. The rhythm of brushing felt soothing, like drawing careful lines across a soft canvas.

She shifted to Willow's other side. The mare stepped over willingly, allowing access.

"You are such a good girl," Emma murmured.

Willow snorted softly and lowered her head.

Emma brushed along her neck, then down her legs. She was careful to move slowly, announcing each change of position with a soft murmur. Willow responded with relaxed ears and a steady breath.

Jake's voice suddenly echoed down the aisle. "Someone is in horse spa mode."

Emma glanced back to see him leaning against the door, rain dripping from his hair.

"What happened to your umbrella?" Emma asked.

"It got sacrificed to the wind," Jake said solemnly. "I will remember it fondly."

Emma laughed. "Marlene said I could groom Willow today."

Jake stepped closer, keeping his hands at his sides to avoid startling the mare. "Wow. That is like being given a magical sword in an adventure story."

Emma raised an eyebrow. "A magical sword."

"Yes. The one only the chosen person can wield."

"Why would Willow be a sword?"

Jake shrugged. "I am brainstorming metaphors."

Emma shook her head, but she was smiling.

Jake leaned against the frame. "But seriously, Willow does not bond with many people. This is cool."

Willow lifted her head and sniffed the air near Jake.

"Hey, girl," he said softly. "I did not bring treats today, so do not look at me like that."

Willow flicked her tail in response.

Jake grinned. "She likes you better anyway."

Emma brushed Willow's shoulder again, her heart glowing. "I hope so."

"You should," Jake said. "Because she totally does."

After finishing with the soft brush, Emma used a clean cloth to wipe Willow's face gently. The mare stood perfectly still, letting Emma clean around her eyes and nose.

"You are amazing," Emma whispered.

Willow's breath warmed Emma's cheek.

When the grooming was finished, Emma took a step back and

admired the mare. Willow's coat shone beautifully, even in the rainy light coming from the barn windows.

Marlene returned with a small smile. "She looks wonderful."

"Thank you," Emma said, brushing a stray hair from her forehead. "She was very calm."

"She trusts you," Marlene said. "That is special."

Before Emma could respond, a sudden metallic clang came from the back of the barn. The same sharp, startling sound that had frightened Willow the day before.

Willow jerked her head up immediately. Her ears pricked sharply toward the noise. Her muscles tensed beneath her glossy coat.

Emma felt her own breath hitch.

"It is okay," she said softly. "You are all right."

Willow snorted and pawed at the ground but did not step back. Emma placed a steady hand on the mare's neck, keeping her voice low.

"It is only a bucket. Nothing scary. You are all right."

Willow blew out a tense breath. Emma gently stroked her neck. The mare's muscles slowly softened.

Marlene nodded with approval. "You handled that well."

Emma swallowed. "I remembered what you said."

"Good." Marlene stepped aside as Tom, the stable manager, appeared holding the offending bucket.

"Sorry for the scare," Tom said. "It slipped. Again."

Jake groaned. "Those buckets have it out for us."

Tom shrugged. "They are a stubborn bunch."

Willow flicked an ear but stayed quiet.

Emma kept her hand on the mare until she felt Willow relax fully.

"You have a very calming presence," Tom said with a thoughtful nod.

"Thank you," Emma said quietly.

"You should keep working with Willow," he added. "Horses choose their people sometimes. Looks like she chose you."

Emma felt her breath catch. "Really?"

Tom nodded. "Really."

Marlene gave Tom a pointed look. "I was trying not to tell her that yet."

Tom blinked. "Oh. Well. Too late."

Jake snorted with laughter.

Emma's entire chest filled with warm sparks that floated all the way to her fingertips. Willow had chosen her. Not Riley. Not anyone else. Her.

She did not quite know what to do with that information.

Willow nudged her shoulder gently, as if confirming the truth.

Once the excitement settled, Emma helped Marlene with a few more chores. They refolded saddle pads, organized grooming supplies, and carried buckets to the tack room. The cozy sound of rain continued outside, turning the stable yard into a soft gray mirror.

After the chores were finished, Marlene approached her with a gentle look. "Emma, I want you to join us for a short groundwork session with Willow tomorrow. Only if you want to."

Emma's heart skipped. "Groundwork. Like leading her around the arena."

"Yes," Marlene said. "And helping her practice listening skills. It is important for riders to understand horses from the ground before taking the next step."

Emma could hardly breathe. "Can I really."

Marlene nodded. "I trust you."

Emma blinked. "Thank you."

Her mother arrived to pick her up soon after, umbrella in hand and a warm smile on her face.

"How was it?" she asked as Emma climbed into the car.

Emma hesitated, unsure how to explain the full weight of what she felt. "It was... really good."

Her mom gave her a knowing look. "I am glad."

On the drive home, the rain slowed to a gentle mist. Through the car window, the fields and fences looked peaceful. A few horses stood under their shelters, tails swishing lazily.

Emma leaned her forehead against the cool window and smiled softly.

Willow had chosen her.

She could not stop thinking about it. The idea felt huge, like she had been handed something precious and rare that she needed to protect.

When they reached home, Emma ran upstairs and sat on her bed, hugging her pillow. The house felt warmer than usual. Her room no longer felt strange or temporary.

She closed her eyes and remembered Willow's breathing, the warm brush of her muzzle, the way the mare had leaned into her grooming.

That memory settled around her like a blanket.

She finally lay back and let herself believe it all.

She was not just adjusting to Saddle Creek.

She was beginning to belong here.

And Willow was becoming part of her story in a way she had never expected.

Later that night, Emma stood at her window again. The trees in the backyard swayed gently in the soft breeze. The moon glowed behind the clouds, giving everything a silvery sheen.

She listened.

The forest was quiet.

Then, just as she was about to shut the window, she heard something faint and distant. A soft sound, almost like a whimpering call. Not quite a whinny. Not quite a bark. Something in between.

Emma leaned forward.

The sound faded.

A chill traced down her back, though she did not feel scared. She felt curious. Slightly unsettled. A little worried. And strangely expectant, as if something out there was watching or waiting.

She placed her hand on the glass.

"What is that?" she whispered.

No answer came.

But she could not shake the feeling that whatever it was, Willow had heard it too.

Emma let the curtain fall back into place and climbed into bed. Willow's soft breath and warm presence drifted through her thoughts until she fell asleep.

Outside, the forest settled under the gentle rain.

And something small, hidden deep within the trees, cried again.

Very softly.

Very alone.

But tomorrow would bring new light.

And Emma would step closer than ever to the truth, whether she meant to or not.

Chapter Six

The sun peeked shyly over the tops of the pine trees the next morning, casting lines of soft light across the fields that surrounded Saddle Creek Stables. The grass glimmered with leftover dew, and a thin fog clung near the ground, curling around the fences like pale ribbons. Emma breathed in the fresh morning air as her mom pulled the car into the parking area.

Today was the groundwork session with Willow.

Her stomach fluttered with a mix of excitement and nerves. She had hardly slept. Every time she closed her eyes, she imagined leading Willow around the arena, feeling her respond, feeling that quiet connection grow deeper and steadier. She wanted to do well. She wanted to prove that yesterday had not been a lucky moment.

Most of all, she wanted Willow to trust her.

Her mom leaned across the front seat and gave her a gentle squeeze on the hand. "Enjoy it. And remember to breathe."

Emma grinned weakly. "I will."

She stepped out of the car. The early air wrapped around her like a cool blanket. A crow cawed somewhere near the woods, breaking the stillness.

Inside the barn, the morning hum had already begun. Riders filled water buckets. Someone swept the aisle with long, confident strokes. Hooves shifted inside stalls. A few horses poked their heads out, ears flicking curiously at Emma as she passed.

Pepper nickered softly. Maple stretched his neck toward her as if expecting a treat. Stormwatch snorted in his usual fierce but dignified way. Emma smiled and greeted each horse quietly.

Then she reached Willow's stall.

The chestnut mare stood near the back, her head lowered as she nibbled at a fresh flake of hay. When Emma whispered her name, Willow lifted her head immediately, ears pricked and eyes bright with recognition.

Emma's heart melted. "Hi, girl."

Willow stepped closer, her breath warm against Emma's hand.

Jake appeared from behind a stack of saddle pads with his usual energy bolting ahead of him. "There she is. The Willow Whisperer."

Emma laughed. "Please do not call me that."

"Too late." Jake grinned proudly. "It is already your official barn nickname."

"Please do not tell Riley," Emma said.

Jake paused. "Yeah. That is fair. She would absolutely use that against you."

Emma rolled her eyes. "Probably."

Jake hopped onto an overturned tack box and sat like he was a king on a throne. "So, ready for your first real groundwork lesson with the mighty Willow."

Emma nodded. "I think so."

"Good. And for the record," Jake said, pointing at Willow, "she is in an unusually good mood this morning."

Willow flicked an ear at him as if acknowledging his statement.

Before Emma could respond, Marlene walked over holding a lead rope and a training stick. "Good morning, Emma. And Jake, the feed shed needs sweeping."

Jake sighed theatrically. "I was hoping you would forget."

"I never forget chores," Marlene said with a raised eyebrow.

Jake hopped off the tack box. "Fine. But if the feed bags fall on me again, I am haunting this barn forever."

"Noted," Marlene replied without looking back.

When Jake disappeared around the corner, Marlene turned to Emma. "All right. Ready to work with Willow."

Emma ran a hand along Willow's neck. "Yes."

"Good. First we groom her. Calmly. No rush."

Emma retrieved the grooming kit and stepped into the stall. Willow relaxed instantly. Emma brushed her slowly and methodically. The mare's breathing grew steady. She occasionally shifted position to give Emma better access to her favorite spots.

"You two look very peaceful together," Marlene said softly, watching from the door.

Emma felt warmth spread through her chest. "She makes it easy."

After the grooming was finished, Marlene clipped on the lead rope and handed it to Emma. "Walk with her to the arena. Let her walk beside you, not behind you. And do not tug. Just guide her with your body."

Emma swallowed her nerves and nodded.

She opened the stall door. Willow followed immediately, her hooves making soft thuds on the concrete floor. Emma kept her hand steady near the clip and walked forward with slow, purposeful steps.

Willow walked beside her with perfect calm.

"I knew she would do well with you," Marlene said.

They reached the training arena. The sand was slightly damp from last night's drizzle but still soft and level. The air smelled fresh and clean.

Marlene locked the gate behind them and stood near the center. "All right. Begin by leading her around the rail. Keep your shoulders relaxed. Try to feel her energy through the rope."

Emma nodded, took a breath, and walked forward. Willow followed closely, ears tipped toward Emma. Each step felt like a conversation. Emma shortened the lead slightly, and Willow responded. She changed direction gently when Emma turned left. She slowed when Emma slowed.

After a few minutes, Marlene called, "Excellent. Now let us try sending her out in a small circle."

Emma hesitated. "Sending her out?"

"Yes. Step slightly to the side and point with your free hand. Use your body to ask her to move around you."

Emma tried. She stepped sideways, pointed with her hand, and gave a small cluck with her tongue. Willow blinked, shifted her weight, and then began stepping outward into a loose circle.

Emma could hardly believe it.

"She is listening to you very carefully," Marlene said. "You have a quiet energy. Horses like quiet energy."

Emma felt something warm spread in her chest. She worked with Willow through circles, halts, backing up, and direction changes. Willow responded to nearly every cue, sometimes before Emma even realized she had asked for it.

It felt magical.

Eventually, Marlene clapped her hands lightly. "Very good. Give her a break and bring her back in."

Emma walked to Willow and stroked her neck. The mare lowered her head and pressed it gently against Emma's chest. Emma giggled softly and wrapped her arms around her neck.

"I love you too," Emma whispered.

Marlene made a quiet sound of approval. "You two really are a perfect pair."

Emma was glowing.

Until everything went wrong.

Jake returned to the arena carrying a bucket and wearing a guilty expression.

"Do not be mad," he said, approaching cautiously. "But there is a situation."

Marlene sighed as if she had predicted this. "What happened."

Jake held up the bucket. "So I was trying to carry two buckets and a rake at the same time and also open the feed room door with my foot. I guess I misjudged my coordination because the rake swung the wrong way and knocked over a whole stack of metal scoops. Those scoops are loud when they hit concrete. Very loud. Like, ridiculously loud."

Emma winced. "Oh no."

"And I might have scared Stormwatch, who then scared Pepper, who then knocked over the broom, and somehow the broom knocked the feed chart off the wall. It was a chain reaction."

Marlene pinched the bridge of her nose. "Jake."

Jake held up one finger. "But here is the good news. Nothing broke. And nobody died."

"That is hardly a reassurance," Marlene said dryly.

Willow's ears had been flicking in Jake's direction the entire time he spoke. Now she snorted with suspicion.

Jake laughed nervously. "Do not worry, Willow. I am done causing chaos for the morning."

Emma smiled awkwardly. "You sure."

"Well, probably."

Before anyone could continue, Lisa, one of the younger riders, ran up to the arena fence.

"Jake," she yelled breathlessly. "Your prank is happening. The one you set up earlier. The rubber snake. It fell into the water trough and freaked everyone out."

Jake went pale. "Wait, which rubber snake. The green one or the big brown one."

"The big brown one," Lisa said. "The one that looks almost real."

Jake dropped the bucket. "Oh no. That was not supposed to fall. That was a joke for you, Lisa, not for the horses."

"I screamed," Lisa said.

"I would have too," Jake admitted. "But that snake is not supposed to be anywhere near the horses. If Stormwatch sees it, he will launch himself into orbit."

"We have to get it before anyone else sees," Lisa said.

Jake sprinted across the yard.

Marlene looked like she wanted to yell, but she sighed instead. "We will talk about consequences later," she murmured.

Willow, watching all the commotion, lifted her head sharply.

"Easy, girl," Emma said gently.

Willow flicked her tail and pawed the ground anxiously. Emma moved closer to her, but Willow's eyes were already fixed on something outside the arena.

"Emma, step in front of her," Marlene said calmly.

Emma obeyed.

Willow's ears pinned forward. She snorted loudly and shifted backward.

Something had spooked her.

Not the snake prank. It was too far away. Something else.

Emma felt the lead rope tighten as Willow backed away again.

"It is okay, Willow," Emma whispered.

But the mare's muscles quivered. She stepped sideways abruptly.

Emma tried to guide her back, but Willow pulled harder. Panic flashed across the mare's eyes. Emma felt her own breath hitch.

Then something clattered loudly near the barn. It sounded like someone had knocked over a stack of metal grooming pails.

Willow reared slightly, startled.

Emma lost her footing.

The lead rope yanked forward out of her hands.

Emma stumbled and fell to her knees. Sand filled her palms. She gasped and scrambled to get up, but Willow backed farther away, nostrils flaring, eyes wide with fear.

"Willow," Emma cried. She reached for the rope again, but it was just out of reach.

Marlene stepped forward immediately. "Willow, stand."

Willow froze, trembling. Emma's heart hammered in her chest as she rose shakily to her feet.

"Emma, move slowly," Marlene instructed. "Do not run toward her."

Emma swallowed and took a cautious step. Willow flicked her eyes toward her voice. Emma lowered her hands and spoke softly.

"It is okay, girl. I am here."

Willow's breathing slowed slightly.

Emma reached for the rope again and this time her fingers brushed the braided cotton. She grabbed it gently.

"It is all right," she whispered. "I am here."

Willow lowered her head into Emma's chest and trembled against her.

Emma stroked her neck, feeling her own nerves begin to settle.

Marlene joined them. "Very good, Emma. You did not panic. That is important."

Emma's legs felt weak. "She almost ran."

"But she did not," Marlene said. "Because you called her back."

Emma let out a shaky breath.

Jake jogged back to the arena holding a soaking wet rubber snake.

"Crisis averted," he announced. "Nobody died. Except maybe the snake."

He saw Emma's pale face and froze. "What happened."

"Willow spooked," Marlene said. "Twice."

Jake's eyes widened. "Is she okay."

"She is," Emma said. She brushed a tear she had not realized had escaped. "But she got scared."

Jake looked guilty. "Was it because of the snake."

"No," Marlene replied. "Something else."

Emma glanced toward the woods. The far tree line shimmered slightly in the heat. A faint sound, almost like a soft yelp, drifted through the air. Emma strained to hear it.

Willow's ears turned sharply toward the trees.

The sound stopped.

. . .

After the incident, Emma walked Willow cautiously back to the barn. The mare stayed close, her shoulder brushing Emma's as if asking for reassurance.

Emma stroked her neck, still feeling rattled. Willow had scared her, but the fear had mostly come from the worry that Willow might hurt herself, not from the horse herself.

Together they entered the barn aisle. The quiet was comforting.

Emma led Willow into her stall and unclipped the lead rope. Willow immediately pressed her head gently against Emma's chest, a gesture so tender that Emma nearly cried again.

"You scared me," Emma whispered into her mane. "But I am here."

Willow blew warm breath against her shoulder.

Marlene approached from the doorway. "She is calm with you. That tells me everything."

Emma nodded shakily.

Jake stood behind Marlene with a drenched shirt from the trough fiasco. He looked nervous. "Emma, I did not mean to make the day crazy. I really did not."

"I know," Emma said.

"And if I caused the noise that spooked her, I am really really sorry."

Emma shook her head. "It was not your prank."

Marlene added, "Something out near the woods made her tense before the pails fell."

Jake frowned. "Again. Like yesterday."

Emma nodded.

A hush settled between them.

Then Marlene clapped her hands gently. "All right. Everyone take a breath. Emma, you did wonderfully. And Willow is fine."

Emma smiled faintly. "Okay."

Marlene placed a hand on her shoulder. "You can take a break now if you want."

Emma stayed beside Willow a moment longer before stepping out of the stall.

Willow whinnied softly at her.

Emma's heart eased.

Her mother arrived a short while later. Emma walked to the car in silence, her mind replaying the moment Willow had pulled away. The moment she had fallen. The moment everything had felt like it was about to explode.

Her mom glanced over once they were on the road. "You are awfully quiet."

"Rough morning," Emma murmured.

"Do you want to talk about it."

Emma stared out the window at the passing fields. "Willow got scared. And I fell. And it just... shook me."

Her mom nodded gently. "Horses get scared sometimes. It does not mean you did anything wrong."

"I know," Emma said, though she did not entirely believe it.

"But she calmed down with you, right." her mom asked.

Emma hesitated. "Yes."

"That means something."

Emma let those words settle.

When they reached home, she went straight to her room. The forest behind the house rustled in the afternoon breeze. A faint sound drifted from far within the trees. Soft. High. Unsettling.

Emma shivered.

Something was out there.

Something Willow had sensed before any of them.

Emma lay down on her bed, still thinking about Willow's trembling body leaning into her.

Today had been scary.

But it had also shown something deeper.
The bond between them was real.
Even when things went wrong.
Especially then.
Outside, the forest whispered again.
And this time, Emma was certain of it.
Something was coming.

Chapter Seven

The next morning arrived with the crispness of early fall, threading cool air through Emma's open window. She woke slowly at first, stretching under her covers, then remembered yesterday's scare and sat up with a jolt. A faint ache still lingered in her knees from when she fell, but the ache was nothing compared to the deeper pinch of worry that had settled in her chest.

She pushed the blankets aside and rattled her thoughts into focus. Today she was going back. Not because she had to. Because she wanted to. Because Willow deserved someone who would not give up on her. And because Emma had felt something in Willow's trembling body yesterday. Trust. Fragile, but real.

Emma rubbed her eyes and dressed quickly, choosing her softest riding pants and a warm hoodie. She tied her hair back in a neat ponytail, took a steadying breath, and headed downstairs.

Her mom stood at the stove flipping pancakes that smelled faintly of cinnamon. The warm scent eased some of the tension in Emma's shoulders.

"Morning," her mom said, turning. "How are you feeling after yesterday."

"A little sore," Emma admitted. "But okay."

Her mom gave her a searching look. "And emotionally."

Emma hesitated. "Nervous. But I want to try again."

"That is brave," her mom said softly. "Sometimes the best moments happen after the scary ones."

Emma nodded, trying to hold on to that truth.

Her dad wandered in a moment later with his hair damp and his reading glasses perched on top of his head in a crooked angle. "Anyone up for pancakes that look like dinosaurs," he asked.

Emma laughed before she could stop herself. "You mean the ones that look like confused turtles and upside down hearts."

Her dad grinned. "Exactly those."

He handed her a plate. Emma took a bite and felt the warmth spread through her entire body. Pancakes were comforting, even when the world felt shaky.

As they drove to the barn, the sky brightened into gentle gold. The tops of the trees glowed with early sunlight, and the road curved neatly between fields still glistening with dew. Emma watched everything pass by her window, thinking of Willow.

Thinking of the moment the mare had rested her head against her chest after the scare. Thinking of how fast her heart had been beating. How quickly she had calmed when Emma whispered to her.

Her mom pulled into the familiar gravel parking area. "Do you want me to walk you in," she asked gently.

"No," Emma said, shaking her head. "I can do it."

Her mom squeezed her shoulder. "I will be close by if you need me."

Emma climbed out of the car and stepped into the cool air. The barn doors were open, sunlight spilling across the entrance like a welcome mat. Birds hopped along the fence posts. Someone in the yard laughed loudly. The world felt alive and safe.

She hoped Willow felt safe today too.

. . .

Inside the barn, the hay scented air felt warm and comforting. Hooves thudded softly in stalls. Riders moved around with arm loads of tack or brushes. The Saturday energy vibrated through the place.

Jake popped into view almost immediately, wearing a straw hat that was very clearly not part of the stable dress code.

"You came back," he said with a relieved grin. "I was worried you might be traumatized forever."

Emma rolled her eyes. "I am fine. Mostly."

"Good. Because Willow has been staring at her stall door all morning like someone is late for her appointment."

Emma's heart fluttered. "Is she okay."

"Seems fine," Jake said. "Jumpy, but not exploding. Which is a good Willow day."

Emma felt a mix of relief and nerves swirl inside her. "Do you think she remembers yesterday."

Jake tilted his head. "Horses remember feelings more than events. If she felt safe with you, she remembers that."

Emma nodded slowly, letting the words sink in.

"Come on," Jake said, lowering his voice dramatically. "The queen awaits."

He led her down the aisle, stopping only to high five a younger rider who was carrying a bucket almost twice her size.

"Whoa, Sarah. You need help with that."

"I got it," Sarah grunted, wobbling down the aisle.

Jake leaned toward Emma and whispered, "Ten bucks says she drops it in front of Maple."

Emma giggled.

They turned the corner.

Willow's stall was halfway down the row, and the moment Emma came into view, Willow lifted her head sharply. Her ears flicked forward with alert interest. Her warm eyes locked onto Emma like she had been waiting for her.

Emma's breath caught. "Hi, girl."

Willow stepped toward the stall door with a soft nicker.

Jake raised both eyebrows. "Yep. She is definitely your horse. Not that she belongs to you," he added quickly, "but she might as well."

Emma stepped closer and let Willow sniff her hand. The mare blew warm breath against her palm and nudged her gently.

"I missed you too," Emma whispered.

Before she could savor the moment, Riley walked up from behind her carrying a bridle and polishing cloth.

"Oh," Riley said, stopping short. "She is being friendly today."

Emma felt her shoulders tense slightly. "Yes. She is calm this morning."

Riley studied Willow with narrowed eyes. "Weird. She is usually more standoffish the day after she spooks."

"Maybe she trusts Emma," Jake said casually, leaning on the stall door.

Riley shot him a look sharp enough to cut through leather. "She trusts people who know what they are doing."

Jake lifted his hands in surrender. "Just saying."

Emma kept her gaze on Willow, focusing on the mare's steady breathing.

Riley softened her tone slightly. "Just be careful today. Willow can act fine one moment and be unpredictable the next."

Emma nodded. "I know."

Riley seemed ready to say something else, but Marlene appeared at the end of the aisle.

"Emma," she called warmly. "Come here, please."

Emma gave Willow one last stroke before jogging toward Marlene.

Marlene smiled gently. "How are you feeling this morning."

"Nervous," Emma admitted. "But excited too."

"That is a healthy combination," Marlene said. "And exactly what you need for today."

Emma swallowed. "What are we doing today."

"Groundwork again," Marlene said. "But this time a little more advanced. I want you to help Willow find her balance again. She depends on you more than you think."

Emma felt something warm bloom in her chest.

Marlene continued. "Go ahead and groom her. Take your time. Pay attention to how she is feeling."

Emma nodded and returned to Willow's stall.

Riley gave her a long, unreadable look before walking away. It was hard to tell whether she was annoyed, curious, jealous, or all three.

Jake leaned in. "I think Riley respects you more after yesterday. In Riley language, that look means she has decided you are not hopeless."

Emma laughed awkwardly. "That is comforting. Sort of."

Jake tapped his straw hat. "See you after chores."

Emma rolled her eyes fondly and stepped into Willow's stall.

Willow stood calmly as Emma brushed her coat in long, soothing strokes. Every so often, Willow nudged her gently as if reminding her that she was there. The mare's trust felt like a fragile glass sculpture that Emma held carefully with both hands.

When she finished grooming, she clipped on the lead rope and gave a soft tug. Willow followed obediently.

Emma led her toward the arena, her nerves fluttering but steady.

Marlene opened the gate for them. "All right. Today we are working on listening, relaxing, and direction changes."

Emma nodded. "Okay."

Willow snorted quietly, ears flicking in alert interest.

Emma walked her along the rail. Willow matched her steps perfectly, her posture relaxed and fluid.

"Good," Marlene said. "Now try a small circle to the left."

Emma stepped sideways. Willow moved smoothly around her in a loose circle. It felt effortless.

"Now change direction."

Emma changed her stance and pointed to the right. Willow switched her weight, turned gracefully, and moved into the opposite circle.

Emma's heart soared. "Good girl."

After several more warm up exercises, Marlene nodded with approval. "She is listening beautifully today."

Emma felt Willow's quiet presence like a warm blanket draped across her shoulders.

"Let us try trot transitions on the line," Marlene said. "Do not push her hard. Just ask lightly. Let her flow into it."

Emma nodded, lifted her hand slightly, and clucked with her tongue.

Willow surged into a smooth trot, her movements rhythmic and controlled.

Emma watched, amazed at how effortlessly Willow responded.

"Keep your energy calm," Marlene reminded her. "Your energy is what she listens to most."

Emma took a deep breath. She imagined her mind melting into a calm pool, still and steady. Willow's trot slowed without Emma asking.

"Very good," Marlene said. "Now bring her back in."

Emma stepped toward Willow and lowered her hand. Willow slowed to a walk and approached Emma willingly, lowering her head for a soft nuzzle.

"You did so well," Emma whispered.

Willow exhaled a long, satisfied breath.

Marlene approached with a quiet smile. "Emma, I am going to say something important. You are ready to ride Willow at a walk today."

Emma's heart jumped. "Really."

"Yes," Marlene said. "Just for a little while. Only if Willow seems relaxed, and only at a walk. But you have earned this."

Emma's face warmed with joy. "Thank you."

Marlene placed a hand on her shoulder. "You and Willow have

something special. But you must remember something. Riding is a conversation. Do not speak too loudly. Willow likes whisperers."

Emma nodded with solemn understanding.

Jake met them outside the arena with a handful of maple leaves that had fallen nearby. "Emma, check this out. I found a leaf shaped like a chicken."

Emma squinted at it. "How is that a chicken."

"It has wings."

"It has points."

"Pointy wings."

"Jake," Emma said, unable to hide her smile, "it looks like a triangle with extra triangles."

Jake gasped dramatically. "You insult the art of nature."

Emma laughed, and the tension in her belly loosened.

Marlene returned with a simple English saddle and bridle. "Let us tack her up gently."

Emma helped buckle the girth, making sure it was neither too loose nor tight. Willow shifted occasionally, but remained calm.

When everything was ready, Emma led Willow into the arena again. The world seemed to go quiet except for the soft hum of air through the trees.

Emma swallowed. "What do I do first."

"Walk her to the mounting block," Marlene instructed. "Let her stand beside it. Then swing your leg carefully over her back. Do not rush."

Emma nodded and guided Willow to the block. The mare stood with her ears relaxed and her tail hanging gently.

Emma stepped onto the block.

Her heart beat hard enough that she wondered if Willow could hear it.

She placed her left foot in the stirrup. Willow stayed still.

Emma inhaled slowly, swung her leg over, and settled into the saddle.

She felt Willow's warmth beneath her. Felt her muscles shift softly. Felt a wave of calm sweep through her entire body.

Marlene stepped to the center of the arena. "Take your time. Let Willow feel your balance."

Emma straightened her posture. Willow shifted once, then settled.

"Now, when you are ready," Marlene said, "ask her to walk."

Emma tightened her legs gently.

Willow moved.

A simple, calm walk. Smooth and steady.

Emma inhaled sharply. "Oh my gosh," she whispered.

Willow's ears flicked back toward her, listening.

Emma smiled in disbelief.

She was riding Willow.

For the next ten minutes, she walked Willow around the small arena, turning gently, changing direction, stopping quietly, and letting the mare listen to every cue.

It felt like floating.

It felt like flying without leaving the ground.

It felt right.

Marlene clapped softly. "Beautiful work. That is enough for today. End on a good note."

Emma brought Willow to a soft halt and dismounted carefully. Willow lowered her head toward her in calm acceptance.

"You were amazing," Emma whispered, embracing her neck.

Willow breathed against her hair.

After untacking Willow and brushing her cool coat, Emma escorted her back to the stall. Willow paused before stepping inside and pressed her forehead softly into Emma's shoulder.

Emma closed her eyes, touched beyond words.

"You two look like you share secrets," Jake said from the aisle.

Emma blinked. "Hi. How long were you standing there."

"Long enough to realize Willow loves you," Jake said with a sincere tone that caught Emma off guard.

Riley appeared behind him. "She was decent today."

Jake smirked. "High praise from Riley."

Riley ignored him. She looked at Emma with a strange mix of respect and conflict.

"You did well," Riley said simply.

Emma blinked. "Thank you."

Riley nodded once, then walked away.

Jake watched her leave. "That is practically a love letter from Riley."

Emma shook her head. "Stop."

Jake grinned.

When Emma got home, she felt light. Not weightless, but steady, anchored, in a way she had not felt since moving to Saddle Creek.

She spent the evening reading beside the window. Every so often, she would glance toward the forest, watching the shadows of tree branches dance in the wind.

Near bedtime, she heard it again.

A faint cry.

Not quite a whinny. Not quite a howl.

Soft. Weak. Almost pleading.

She stepped closer to the window and listened hard.

Silence.

Then, barely audible, the sound came again.

Emma pressed her hand against the glass.

Something was out there.

Something alone.

Something small.

She swallowed and stepped back from the window.

Tomorrow she would see Willow again.

Tomorrow she would learn more.

Tomorrow the forest might whisper again.

And slowly, very slowly, the pieces of something bigger were sliding into place.

Emma had no idea how much her life was changing.

But Willow knew.

And soon, Emma would too.

Chapter Eight

The morning of Emma's next lesson arrived wrapped in a soft chill that hinted at the season shifting. She woke to faint sunlight filtering through her curtains, painting long gold bars across her bedroom floor. The quiet felt different today, heavier somehow, as if the air itself sensed she was on the verge of something important. Emma lay still for a moment, listening to the rustle of the trees outside and the faint hum of the waking world. She was nervous. More nervous than she had expected. The memory of the previous day, riding Willow at a walk, still glowed inside her like a warm ember. But so did the sudden jolt of fear from the day before that, when Willow had spooked so sharply she had almost dragged Emma off her feet. That memory slid into her thoughts now like a cold shadow, chilling the warm parts of her courage.

She dressed slowly, choosing clothes more carefully than usual. Pulling her riding pants on felt like an act of bravery, as if each piece of gear was armor she hoped would protect her against uncertainty. She brushed her hair back, tied it neatly, and stared at her reflection for a long moment. She looked like a rider. That comforted her. But the fluttering in her stomach reminded her that looking like a rider and feeling like one were not the same thing.

Downstairs, the scent of scrambled eggs drifted through the house. Her father was stirring a pan while humming quietly, and her mother sat at the kitchen table with a warm mug of coffee cupped in her hands. Her eyes softened the moment she saw Emma come down the stairs. "Good morning, sweetheart," she said gently. "You look tired. Did you sleep all right."

Emma shrugged and reached for a glass of juice. "Mostly. I kept waking up thinking about today."

Her father glanced over his shoulder with an expression both sympathetic and proud. "Being nervous means it matters to you. That is not a bad thing."

Emma nodded, though it did not ease the knot in her stomach. Her mother reached across the table and squeezed her hand. "You handled Willow beautifully last time. No matter what happens today, you should be proud of yourself."

Emma swallowed the lump in her throat. "I want to do well," she said softly. "But I do not want Willow to get scared again."

"Willow trusts you," her mom said. "Trust her too. You are building something special together."

Her dad set the plate of eggs on the table and sat, but Emma could barely force herself to eat. She managed a few bites, washed them down with a gulp of juice, and tried to convince her stomach that food was a good idea. After breakfast, she grabbed her helmet and zipped her jacket up to her chin.

The drive to Saddle Creek Stables was quiet. Her parents seemed to understand that she did not want to talk much. She stared out the window at the passing trees and tried to calm her thoughts. The morning light made everything look peaceful. Horses grazed in paddocks near the road, swishing their tails lazily. Birds hopped along the fence posts. Even the clouds, light and fluffy and drifting slowly, seemed relaxed.

She wished she felt as calm.

When the car turned into the gravel parking area, Emma's heart began to thump. The barn came into view, red roof shining, white fences stretching across the fields. She loved the sight. Yet today it looked taller, larger, heavier somehow, as if the barn itself knew what she was afraid of.

Her mom parked and turned in her seat. "Do you want me to walk with you."

Emma shook her head. "No. I think I should go in alone."

She reached for the door handle, paused, then leaned across to hug her mom. "Wish me luck."

"You do not need luck," her mom whispered. "You just need to be yourself."

Emma stepped out of the car and inhaled deeply. The crisp morning air filled her lungs, cooling her nerves a little. She squared her shoulders and headed for the barn.

Inside, the familiar sounds greeted her. Horses shifting in their stalls. Hooves scraping lightly. The soft rumble of contented snorts. Riders chatting near the tack room. The scent of hay and leather wrapped around her in a way that always made her feel safe.

She had taken only a few steps down the aisle when Jake appeared in front of her, holding a broom like a sword and wearing a bright grin. "Well look who showed up ready to conquer the world," he said dramatically. "Emma the Brave, returning to the scene of yesterday's epic victory."

Emma laughed weakly. "I do not feel very brave today."

Jake lowered the broom and studied her face carefully. "Nerves."

"A little," Emma admitted.

Jake leaned on the broom handle. "You know, every rider I have ever met gets nervous. Even Riley. She just pretends she is immune to fear, but I have seen her knees shake before a big show. Real bravery is showing up anyway."

Emma felt some of the tension loosen. "Thanks."

"And speaking of Riley," Jake added, lowering his voice, "she is in a mood today."

Emma blinked. "A good mood or a bad mood."

"Usually when people say someone is in a mood, it means a bad one," Jake said. "And yes. It is that kind."

Emma sighed. "Perfect."

"Do not worry," Jake said. "She does not bite. Probably. And if she does, I will get you a tetanus shot."

Emma snorted. "Helpful."

Jake grinned. "Always."

They walked together toward Willow's stall. Emma's heart thudded harder with each step. She was afraid of being scared again. Afraid of messing up. Afraid Willow would sense her fear.

But when Willow lifted her head and saw Emma, the mare's entire expression changed. Her ears pricked forward. Her eyes softened. She stepped toward the stall door with a soft, welcoming nicker.

Emma exhaled, relief washing through her like a warm wave. "Hi, girl," she whispered, reaching out to stroke Willow's velvety nose through the bars.

Willow nudged her arm gently as though she had been waiting all morning for Emma to arrive.

Jake raised his eyebrows. "Yep. That is love. Pure, unconditional, horsey devotion."

Emma rolled her eyes, but she could not hide her smile.

Riley appeared around the corner with Stormwatch on a lead rope. She halted when she saw Emma, then flicked a glance toward Willow. "She seems unusually calm today," Riley said.

Emma nodded. "She had a good morning, I guess."

Riley studied them for a moment, her expression mixed with curiosity and something else Emma could not identify. "Just do not get too comfortable," Riley said. "Willow can flip from calm to wild with no warning."

Jake whispered, "She means that in a supportive way."

"I did not," Riley said sharply.

Jake smirked.

Riley rolled her eyes and continued down the aisle with Stormwatch, muttering something under her breath about boys with too many opinions.

Emma focused back on Willow. The mare looked peaceful and relaxed, but Emma still felt the nervous flutter inside her chest. She wished she could turn off fear the way some riders seemed to do naturally. She wished she felt as confident as Willow looked.

Marlene appeared just then, holding a saddle pad and a clipboard. "Emma," she said warmly. "Good morning. How are you feeling."

Emma swallowed. "A little nervous."

"That is completely normal," Marlene said gently. "Especially after a scare. Today we will ease into things. No rushing."

Emma nodded gratefully.

"Go ahead and groom Willow," Marlene said. "Take your time. Read her mood."

Emma stepped into Willow's stall, brushing the mare gently in long strokes across her glossy coat. Willow relaxed instantly, her breathing slow and steady. Emma moved carefully, checking for any tension or signs of discomfort. Willow shifted slightly to give her access to her favorite spots, and Emma felt herself breathing more evenly as the grooming continued.

When she finished, Marlene helped her tack up Willow. The mare stayed calm through the entire process, which made Emma feel a little more stable inside.

By the time they entered the arena, the sunlight had grown brighter, casting golden beams across the pale sand. Dust motes drifted in the light, shimmering like tiny flecks of magic.

Marlene set the mounting block in place. "We will start with a relaxed walk again. Nothing more unless Willow feels soft and steady."

Emma nodded and placed her foot in the stirrup. Her heart hammered, but she swung her leg over Willow's back carefully. Once in the saddle, she settled slowly, letting her body adjust.

Willow shifted her weight once, then stood still.

Emma breathed out. "Okay," she whispered.

"Good," Marlene said from the center of the arena. "Now gently ask her to walk."

Emma squeezed lightly with her legs. Willow stepped forward with her usual smoothness. Emma focused on the sound of Willow's hooves, the rhythm of the saddle, the sway of the mare's body. Step by step, her nerves softened into something calmer.

"Nicely done," Marlene said. "Let her warm up in both directions."

Emma guided Willow around the arena, changing direction every so often. Willow remained steady, ears relaxed, tail swinging naturally. Emma felt her own breathing fall into rhythm with the mare's movement.

After a few minutes, Marlene called out, "Very good. Now let us try a little trot. Only if you feel ready."

The nerves immediately darted back into Emma's stomach. She bit her lip. The last time she had trotted on Willow, things had gone fine, but today she felt fragile.

She hesitated.

"Emma," Marlene said gently, "you do not have to trot today. Your confidence matters more than the pace you ride at."

Emma swallowed hard. "I want to try," she whispered.

"Only try," Marlene reminded her. "Not push."

Emma nodded. She squeezed Willow gently.

Willow lifted her head a fraction, flicked her ears back at Emma's cue, and started trotting.

The first bounce startled Emma. She rose into a posting rhythm, but she was slightly off beat. She adjusted, posting higher, then lower, trying to match Willow's stride.

Willow trotted calmly, but Emma felt her balance wavering. Her knees bounced awkwardly against the saddle. Her left foot slipped slightly in the stirrup.

Panic flashed through her.

Willow sensed it.

The mare's ears snapped backward, listening for tension.

Emma's heart lurched. Her body stiffened. Willow shifted under her, trying to understand the sudden fear.

Emma lost her posting rhythm. She tipped forward.

Willow spooked at the change in balance, darting sideways unexpectedly.

Emma felt the world tilt.

She clutched the reins too tight.

Her foot slipped entirely from one stirrup.

Then she felt herself falling.

Time slowed, stretching into a drawn out moment. Emma twisted, trying desperately to stay on. Her hands slipped. Her balance tipped. She slid sideways.

Her heart slammed against her ribs.

She braced for impact.

But Willow stopped abruptly, planting her feet firmly as if trying to catch Emma with her stillness. The sudden halt nearly threw Emma forward, but she managed to grab Willow's mane and cling tightly.

Her breath tore out of her in a ragged gasp.

Willow trembled under her.

Emma trembled too.

Marlene was at her side in an instant, one hand steadying Willow's bridle and the other reaching for Emma's leg. "Breathe," she said calmly. "Let me take your reins. You are okay."

Emma's whole body shook. Her eyes stung. Her lungs felt tight, barely able to pull in air.

"You did not fall," Marlene said softly. "You stayed on. Willow stopped for you."

Emma slid shakily out of the saddle with Marlene's help. As soon as her boots touched the ground, her knees buckled and she collapsed against Willow's neck, burying her face in the mare's warm coat. Tears spilled before she could stop them.

"I am sorry," she whispered, her voice cracking. "I was scared. I did not mean to make you nervous."

Willow exhaled softly, brushing her muzzle against Emma's shoulder. The mare's breath felt like a soft apology. Or maybe reassurance.

Marlene placed a gentle hand on Emma's back. "You did nothing wrong. Horses feel our emotions. Willow reacted to your fear, not your mistakes. She stayed with you."

Emma sniffed hard. "I almost fell."

"But you did not," Marlene reminded her. "And even more important, you listened to your instincts. You slowed down. You stopped when you needed to."

Emma wiped her eyes. She felt small and embarrassed, but also relieved. Her heart was still pounding painfully, though it was slowly returning to normal.

Jake appeared at the arena fence, eyes wide with concern. "What happened. Are you okay."

Emma nodded weakly. "Almost fell."

Jake frowned. "Emma, that is terrifying. But you are still alive, which means you did better than half the people who ride for the first time on Willow."

Emma managed a tiny laugh.

Riley appeared beside him. "Did she fall."

"No," Jake said.

Riley exhaled, relief flickering briefly across her features before she masked it. "Good."

Emma felt touched by the tiny moment of unexpected softness.

Marlene turned to both of them. "Give Emma some space, please."

They stepped back obediently.

Marlene guided Willow and Emma to the mounting block. "I want you to take a moment holding the reins again, just standing. No riding. No pressure. I want Willow to end this experience with calm energy."

Emma nodded shakily.

She stood beside Willow, holding the reins lightly. Willow's breathing steadied. Emma's breathing slowly matched it.

After a few minutes, Emma whispered, "Thank you, girl. I know I scared you. But you tried to help me. I felt it."

Willow blinked and pressed her forehead gently against Emma's arm.

Marlene smiled softly. "You two are learning to trust each other. Trust is not built on perfect days. It is built on days exactly like this."

Emma looked up at her, surprised.

Marlene continued, "You did not quit. You did not blame Willow. You stayed present. That is what makes a good rider."

Emma nodded, though she still felt shaky.

"Take her back to the barn," Marlene said. "Walk slowly. Let yourselves settle."

Emma led Willow out of the arena. Her legs trembled, but she held her head high. Willow walked beside her calmly, occasionally brushing her shoulder against Emma's as if checking she was still there.

Inside the barn, Emma brushed Willow carefully, her strokes soft and slow. Willow relaxed fully, lowering her head until her muzzle nearly touched Emma's chest.

Jake hovered nearby, pretending to organize grooming tools while stealing worried glances at her. "If you need to cry again, I will cry with you," he said quietly.

Emma let out a watery laugh. "I am okay. Just embarrassed."

"You should not be," Jake said firmly. "You stayed on Willow. That is something even Riley has not managed every time."

Riley, who had been pretending not to listen, cleared her throat loudly. "I heard that."

"It is true," Jake said.

Riley crossed her arms. "Falling is part of riding. Everyone falls at some point. You did not even fall. So do not start thinking you are weak."

Emma blinked at her. "Are you trying to be nice."

Riley groaned. "I am being realistic."

Jake leaned toward Emma and whispered, "This is what nice looks like for Riley."

Emma nodded.

When Emma finished untacking and grooming Willow, she hugged the mare one last time. "See you tomorrow," she whispered.

Willow nickered softly, the sound warm and reassuring.

The drive home felt longer than usual. Emma stared out the window, replaying the moment she lost her balance. Her stomach twisted each time she thought about almost falling. She felt ashamed. Disappointed. Afraid.

When they arrived home, Emma headed straight to her room and curled up on her bed. She hugged her pillow tightly and let the tears fall again, quietly this time.

She fell asleep like that, exhausted.

She woke later to the soft sound of the wind moving through the trees. Dusk had fallen, painting her room in muted shades of purple and gray. Something in the air felt strange, heavy with a quiet she could not quite explain.

She stood and walked to her window, pressing her palms to the cool glass.

The forest looked mysterious and shadowed, the trees shifting gently in the fading light.

Then she heard it.

A soft cry.

High pitched. Lonely. Fragile.

Her breath caught.

She leaned closer.

The sound came again, barely audible but unmistakably real.

Something was out there in the depths of the trees.

Something scared.

Something small.

Emma shivered and stepped back.

Whatever it was, the horses sensed it.

Willow sensed it.

And now Emma sensed it too.

Tomorrow she would go back to the barn.

Tomorrow she would try again.

But tonight, as the shadows deepened and the forest whispered its strange cry again, Emma realized that her life at Saddle Creek was growing far bigger and more mysterious than she had ever imagined.

Chapter Nine

The day after Emma's near fall was bright in a way that felt almost unfair. The sky was clear and blue, the air crisp, and the sun shimmered across the dewy fields that stretched around Saddle Creek Stables. Birds darted through the cool morning breeze, chirping energetically as though nothing frightening had happened the day before. But Emma felt the lingering weight of yesterday's fear even as she walked toward the barn.

Her boots crunched through a thin layer of gravel. The barn doors were already open, and the early morning rush was underway. Riders were grooming horses, filling buckets, hauling tack, or sweeping the aisles. The smell of hay mixed with the scent of warm grain and freshly polished leather. Normally that atmosphere comforted Emma. Today it only tightened the knot in her stomach.

She glanced toward Willow's paddock and felt her chest squeeze. Willow stood near the fence with her head lowered, grazing quietly, her chestnut coat glowing in the sunlight. Emma raised a hand to wave, but the mare did not look up. For some reason, that small detail worried Emma more than the idea of mounting a horse again.

She stepped inside the barn, scanning the aisle for Marlene or

Jake. She found Jake sitting on a hay bale near the grooming stalls, eating what looked like a breakfast bar that was mostly crumbs.

Jake jumped to his feet when he saw her. "Emma. You survived yesterday. That already makes today better."

Emma attempted a smile, but the tension in her stomach made it wobble. "Barely. And today I feel even more nervous."

Jake made a sympathetic face and held up the last piece of his breakfast bar. "Want a bite. It might be stale, but it is emotionally supportive."

Emma shook her head with a small laugh. "Thanks, but I think you need that more than I do."

"Fair," Jake said, popping it into his mouth.

Before Emma could say more, Marlene appeared from behind a stack of tack trunks. She held a clipboard and wore a thoughtful expression. "Good morning, Emma. How are you feeling."

"Still scared," Emma admitted.

"That is normal," Marlene said. "The important thing is that you came back. Courage is not about feeling unafraid. It is about continuing in spite of fear." She gestured toward Willow's paddock. "You do not have to ride today unless you want to. But we should work on confidence from the ground again. A trusting partnership is built step by step."

Emma nodded. "I want to try groundwork. Riding can wait."

Marlene smiled approvingly. "Good choice." She pointed toward Willow. "Go bring her in. Take your time with her."

Emma nodded and walked toward the paddock. Each step felt heavy. She replayed the near fall in her mind, the sensation of sliding sideways, the terror rushing through her chest. She shook her head sharply, trying to push the memory away, but it clung to her thoughts like burrs on cloth.

Willow lifted her head as Emma approached, watching her with dark, intelligent eyes. Emma's chest loosened a little. The mare stepped forward, ears relaxed, and exhaled softly against Emma's outstretched hand.

"Hi, girl," Emma whispered. "I missed you."

She clipped on the lead rope and opened the gate. Willow walked beside her calmly, but Emma could not shake the feeling that something fragile inside her was trembling. She wanted to be brave, but she felt thin and stretched, like a thread pulled too tight.

Inside the barn, she led Willow into the grooming stall. The mare shifted her weight slightly but seemed mostly content. Emma began brushing her coat in slow, steady strokes. Willow's eyes softened. The rhythm helped Emma breathe more steadily.

As she brushed Willow's flank, she heard footsteps behind her and stiffened instinctively. She knew who it was before she even turned.

Riley stood there with her arms crossed, wearing a fitted riding jacket, tan breeches, and a guarded expression. Her gaze flicked toward Willow, then back to Emma. She tilted her head slightly and raised an eyebrow. "So you came back."

Emma swallowed. "Yes."

Riley stepped closer, her voice sharp with something that sounded almost like annoyance. "You almost fell yesterday. Hard. I saw it from the arena gate."

"I know," Emma said quietly. "I was there."

Riley rolled her eyes a little. "Obviously. What I mean is that lots of people would have taken a break after something like that. Or switched horses. Maybe you should have."

Emma frowned and brushed Willow's shoulder again. "Why. I like Willow."

Riley exhaled sharply. "That is not the point. Willow is not a beginner horse. She is unpredictable. She spooks at everything. Anyone who has been here longer than a week knows that."

Emma felt a pinch in her chest. "I know she is sensitive. But she likes me."

Riley stiffened, her eyes flashing. "Yes. I noticed."

Emma blinked. The words were not angry, not exactly. They

were tight. Wounded. Defensive. Riley lifted her chin as if daring Emma to comment.

Emma hesitated before saying softly, "I did not do anything to make her like me more."

Riley scoffed. "You do not have to rub it in."

"I am not," Emma said, feeling her own frustration spark. "I love Willow, but I did not steal her from you."

Riley's eyes narrowed. "You would not understand."

"Then explain it," Emma said.

That did it.

Riley's posture stiffened, her shoulders tightening as if bracing for an impact that only she could feel. "I rode Willow before you ever showed up," she snapped. "She used to be my project horse. We trained together for months. But she never responded to me the way she responds to you."

Emma frowned. "Maybe she just needs someone quieter."

Riley's eyes flashed dangerously. "Quieter. So now I am too loud."

"That is not what I meant," Emma said quickly.

"Then what did you mean," Riley demanded, stepping closer. "Because it sounded like you think you are better for her."

Emma felt heat rise in her face. "I do not think I am better. I am just trying to learn."

Riley shook her head. "Willow never listened to me like that. She fought me every step. And now she sees you and suddenly she is calm and perfect and sweet. Like she never needed me at all."

Emma stared at her, surprised at the rawness in Riley's voice. Under the sharp words, she heard something fragile. Something almost painful.

"You care about her," Emma said quietly.

Riley froze for a fraction of a second, her eyes widening before she snapped them into a defensive glare. "Of course I care about her. She was supposed to be my horse. My responsibility. My chance to prove myself. Everyone expected me to work with her. And I tried. Harder than anyone."

Emma lowered her brush. "What happened."

Riley looked away, jaw tight. "She never trusted me enough. Sometimes she got scared and spooked. Sometimes she ignored my cues. Sometimes she acted like she could not stand me. And every time she did that, everyone looked at me like it was my fault."

Emma's breath caught. "I am sorry."

"Do not say that," Riley said sharply, her voice cracking slightly before she forced it into a steady tone. "I do not want your sympathy. I am just telling you why it feels ridiculous that she suddenly acts perfect with you. Like all the months I spent trying to make progress meant nothing."

Emma swallowed hard, unsure how to respond. She felt the sting of guilt even though she knew she had not done anything wrong. "I never meant to take her away from you," she said softly. "I did not know."

Riley crossed her arms tighter. "That is exactly it. You did not have to know. You just walked in and Willow practically rolled out a red carpet for you."

Emma looked down at the ground, her voice quiet. "I am not trying to replace you."

Riley huffed, but her tone softened just barely. "Maybe not. But you did anyway."

The blunt honesty stung. Emma inhaled slowly. "I did not choose it. Willow did."

Riley's expression flickered, showing a crack in her armor. A sliver of hurt mixed with humiliation. She straightened her spine. "I know. And that is the worst part."

"Why," Emma asked.

"Because Willow choosing you means she never chose me," Riley said. "And I do not know how to deal with that."

Emma felt her heart squeeze. "Maybe she needs different things at different times. Maybe she can still learn from you."

Riley shook her head. "You do not get it. People already think I am bossy or too intense or too competitive. When Willow liked me, it proved I could handle tough horses. Without her, I am just another rider with nothing special to show."

"That is not true," Emma said firmly.

Riley looked at her sharply. "You do not know me well enough to say that."

"Maybe not," Emma said, "but I can see you work harder than anyone. I see you helping other riders even when you pretend not to care. I see you trying to push yourself every time. That counts for something."

Riley looked away, her eyes blinking quickly. "You do not understand what it is like to feel like you have to be the best at everything just to prove you deserve to be here."

Emma felt the truth of those words settle heavily between them. Riley was not cruel. She was scared. Scared of being overlooked. Scared of being replaced. Scared that if she was not perfect, she would not matter.

Emma softened her voice. "You do not have to be the best at everything. You just have to be you."

Riley let out a short, humorless laugh. "That is easy for you to say. Willow likes you."

Emma hesitated, then said quietly, "Maybe Willow is not comparing us. Maybe we are the ones comparing us."

Riley's hardened expression wavered. She stared at Emma for a moment, her eyes searching for something she was not sure she wanted to find.

Finally, Riley exhaled. It sounded more like surrender than irritation. "I do not hate you, Emma. I want to. But I do not."

Emma blinked. "I do not hate you either."

Riley nodded slightly. "I know."

There was a long silence.

Then Riley shook her head as if clearing away unwanted thoughts. "Do me a favor."

"What."

"Do not let Willow push you around. She will test you. Hard. And if you do not stand your ground, she will think she has to take care of you instead of you taking care of her."

Emma nodded slowly. "Thank you. I will remember that."

Riley glanced toward Willow and lowered her voice. "And please, do not tell anyone I said any of this. Especially Jake."

Emma nodded immediately. "I will not."

Riley straightened. "Good." Then she turned and walked away, but the tension in her shoulders looked lighter than before.

Emma watched her leave, feeling a strange mix of relief and sadness. Riley was complicated. Hard on the outside, breakable on the inside. But today, for the first time, Emma understood her.

Willow nudged Emma's arm gently, pulling her attention back.

Emma stroked the mare's neck. "You sure know how to cause drama," she whispered.

Willow snorted softly.

Emma finished grooming her and led her into the arena for groundwork. She focused on breathing calmly and speaking with quiet confidence. Willow responded beautifully, matching Emma's cues with fluid grace.

Afterward, Emma walked Willow back to the barn. Jake joined her, carrying a bucket almost half his size.

"I heard voices earlier," Jake said casually. "Anything I should know about."

"No," Emma said quickly. "Just talking."

Jake narrowed his eyes in mock suspicion. "Just talking with Riley. The girl whose eyebrows communicate more judgment than words."

Emma laughed. "She was actually not mean."

Jake nearly dropped the bucket. "What. Are you feeling okay. Should I call a doctor."

Emma rolled her eyes. "Riley is not mean. She is just proud."

"And defensive," Jake added.

"And complicated," Emma said.

"Ah," Jake said thoughtfully. "A barn mystery wrapped in breeches."

Emma nudged him with her elbow. "Stop."

Jake grinned.

When Emma led Willow back into the stall, she stroked her one last time. The mare lowered her head and breathed warm air into Emma's shoulder.

"You will always be special," Emma whispered.

Willow closed her eyes as if she understood.

Emma left the barn feeling light and heavy all at once. She had confronted Riley. She had survived it. And somehow, through the tangle of harsh words and honest truths, she had found a new understanding. Not a friendship yet. But a step toward something better.

That night, when Emma opened her bedroom window, she heard the faint, lonely cry again from the forest. It curled through the trees like a question waiting to be answered. Emma pressed her hand to the sill.

"Soon," she whispered.

And the forest fell quiet once more.

Chapter Ten

Emma woke long before her alarm went off. The room was barely lit, only a faint hint of early morning seeping through her curtains, but her eyes snapped open as though an invisible hand had nudged her awake. For a moment, she lay still, listening to the silence. Her heart was already thumping with a mixture of excitement and fear. Today was show day. Not a big, world changing competition, but a local schooling show held right at Saddle Creek Stables. Still, it was her very first show. Her stomach churned with nerves and anticipation.

She rolled out of bed and peeked through the window. The sky was a dark blue canvas slowly turning softer near the horizon. She could barely make out the tops of the pine trees swaying gently in the early morning breeze. A single bird chirped once, tentatively, like even the wildlife was waking slowly today. Emma pressed her hand against the cool glass. The air outside looked crisp. She hoped Willow was calm.

Her mom knocked softly on the door and pushed it open with a warm smile. "Good morning, sweetheart. Ready for the big day."

"I think so," Emma said, though her voice came out smaller than she intended.

Her mom walked in and sat beside her on the edge of the bed. "Show days are exciting. Nerve wracking, yes. But exciting." Her voice was calm, even cheerful, but it had a steadying quality Emma needed. "You do not have to be perfect today. You do not have to win anything. Just show up and enjoy the moment."

Emma nodded and hugged her pillow to her chest. "I know. I just want Willow to be okay. Shows have a lot going on. People. Loud noises. Decorations. She might get scared."

"That is why she has you," her mom said gently. "Remember, she trusts you."

Emma felt a flutter in her chest. "I really hope so."

"You will be fine," her mom said, brushing a strand of hair away from Emma's face. "Now come downstairs. Your dad made waffles."

Emma changed quickly into riding pants and her Saddle Creek polo shirt. She tied her hair back in a neat ponytail and grabbed her jacket. The smell of warm waffles floating up the stairs helped calm her nerves a little.

Her dad stood at the stove holding a plate of waffles shaped like stars, hearts, and one that looked suspiciously like a dinosaur with a broken tail. "These are good luck waffles," he announced proudly.

Emma laughed, feeling her shoulders loosen. She ate quickly but carefully, knowing a too-full stomach mixed with nerves would be a bad combination. Her parents watched her with soft, encouraging smiles.

The drive to Saddle Creek Stables was quiet but filled with a low electric buzz, the kind of tension that comes right before something important happens. The sun had risen just enough to cast a soft golden glow across the sky. As the car approached the familiar white fences, Emma saw trucks and horse trailers already parked in the gravel lot. Riders walked around in show clothes. Volunteers carried tables, ribbons, and clipboards.

Her heart jumped.

It was really happening.

Her mom squeezed her shoulder as Emma unbuckled her seat belt. "Have a wonderful time. We will be in the stands. Text if you need anything."

Emma nodded, grabbed her gear bag, and stepped out of the car. The cool air hit her face and filled her lungs with something sharp and invigorating.

Saddle Creek buzzed with life. Riders led their horses toward warm up arenas. Parents carried garment bags and water bottles. Someone had hung colorful banners along the fence, and a row of folding chairs lined the main arena. The show announcer tested the speakers with a few gentle taps and static crackles. Volunteers set up tables near the judge's booth, complete with score sheets and a box full of rosettes. The sight made Emma's stomach swoop with nerves.

She made her way inside the barn, where the energy was quieter but still humming. Horses stood in their stalls munching hay, their coats polished until they shone. Riders gathered near the tack room, adjusting jackets, braiding manes, and comparing nerves.

Jake was near the grooming area, standing with his hands on his hips and wearing a very crooked show tie. When he saw Emma, he lit up and waved her over. "Emma. Emergency. Help me. My tie is committing crimes."

Emma laughed. "Hold still." She straightened the tie and tightened the knot. "Who tied this for you."

"Myself," Jake said proudly. "Which, in hindsight, was a terrible idea."

"You think." Emma stepped back and looked at him. "There. Much better."

Jake puffed out his chest. "Watch out world. I am dangerously handsome now."

Emma shook her head with a smile. "You look fine."

Jake glanced at her more seriously. "You ready."

"Terrified," Emma admitted.

"Good," Jake said. "If you were super calm on your first show day, I would assume you were secretly an alien."

Emma laughed again. The tension in her chest eased slightly. "Have you seen Willow yet."

"Yes," Jake said. "And I am happy to report she has not exploded. She seems calm. Weirdly calm. Like creepy calm."

Emma swallowed. "Is that good or bad."

Jake shrugged. "No idea. But Marlene said to bring her in for grooming soon. I think she wants you to do the first bit."

Emma nodded. That made sense. Bonding time before the chaos of the warm up.

She walked down the aisle toward Willow's stall. Each step made her heart thump louder. When she reached the stall, Willow lifted her head immediately. Her ears pricked forward. Her large dark eyes softened.

Emma breathed out slowly. "Hi, girl."

Willow stepped toward the front of the stall with a soft nicker. She exhaled a warm breath against Emma's cheek when she leaned close. Emma stroked her neck gently. "Are you ready. I am really nervous. But you seem calm."

Willow blinked, relaxed and steady.

Emma's heart fluttered with relief. "Okay. We can do this."

She led Willow to the grooming stall. The mare walked beside her with measured steps, quiet and obedient. Emma brushed her coat carefully, each stroke smoothing her own nerves as much as Willow's. Volunteers hurried around the barn hanging schedules and giving riders updates, but Emma focused only on Willow.

Riley appeared a few minutes later wearing her show jacket, hair pulled tightly into a low bun. She looked like she stepped straight out of a riding magazine. Her expression, however, was guarded.

"You look nice," Emma said, hoping it came out friendly.

Riley studied her for a moment. "Thanks. You look fine too."

It was not exactly warm, but it was not an insult. A solid Riley compliment.

Riley approached Willow and raised a hand cautiously. "She looks calm."

Emma nodded. "I think she is in a good mood."

Riley hesitated. Then she said, "I am glad."

Emma blinked. "Really."

Riley rolled her eyes as if annoyed at her own kindness. "I am not rooting for you to fail, if that is what you are thinking."

Emma smiled slightly. "Thanks."

Riley crossed her arms, chewing the inside of her cheek. Then she spoke quietly. "Just be careful in the warm up. Horses can act strange during shows. Willow is smart, but smart horses feel everything. You have to be steady. Even if she is not."

"I will try," Emma said.

Riley nodded and stepped back. "Good."

Jake popped his head around the corner. "Riley is giving advice. Quick. Write it down."

Riley shot him a glare sharp enough to peel paint. "Do you want Stormwatch to step on your shoe."

"Nope," Jake said, disappearing again.

Riley turned back to Emma. "Seriously. Just think about your breathing. Willow mirrors your energy."

Emma nodded firmly. "I will remember that."

Riley hesitated, then walked away before she could say anything else.

When Emma finished grooming Willow, she helped Marlene tack up the mare. The saddle pad was white with a navy trim. The show saddle gleamed with fresh polish. Willow stood perfectly still as the girth tightened, her ears flicking in quiet interest as volunteers shouted about schedules outside.

"Are you ready," Marlene asked gently.

Emma inhaled slowly. "I think so."

"You will be riding her in the walk trot class," Marlene reminded her. "Keep the goals simple. Smooth transitions. Straight lines. Confidence."

Emma nodded.

"Remember, the show is supposed to be fun," Marlene said.

"I will try to have fun," Emma said, though her voice trembled.

Marlene smiled softly. "That is all I want today."

Together they led Willow to the warm up arena. The moment they stepped outside, the energy hit Emma like a gust of wind. People rushed along the fence lines, calling instructions, cheering riders on. Horses pranced or tossed their heads. Announcers spoke over loudspeakers. The judge scribbled notes behind a table covered with scorecards.

Willow tensed immediately. Her head lifted. Her ears flicked rapidly in every direction. Her tail swished in short, irritated motions.

Emma felt her pulse spike. "It is okay, girl," she whispered.

Willow snorted loudly and stepped sideways.

Marlene touched Emma's shoulder. "Walk her slowly around the edge of the arena. Let her see everything."

Emma nodded and took the reins, her hands trembling slightly. She walked forward, Willow circling tightly at first. Emma swallowed her nerves and spoke calmly. "Just look. Everything is fine. I am here."

As they moved, Willow's breathing slowed, and her steps grew longer. She scanned the surroundings but did not bolt or spin.

Emma relaxed a little.

Riley appeared at the rail. "Breathe, Emma. You look like a statue made of fear."

Emma let out a shaky laugh. "Thanks. I needed that."

"Use your corners," Riley said. "Let her look at everything once before you ask her to do anything."

Emma did as she advised. She walked Willow around the warm up several times. Riders trotted in circles, cantered across diagonals, or practiced transitions. No one bumped into each other, but the energy was high and contagious. Willow's ears twitched like antennae picking up every ounce of tension.

Emma focused on staying calm. She remembered Riley's words. Be steady. Even if Willow is not.

And slowly, Willow's movements softened.

"You are doing well," Marlene said as Emma paused near her.

Jake ran over carrying a water bottle. "Good news," he said breathlessly. "No one has fallen off yet. That means we are ahead of schedule."

Emma nodded. "That is great."

Jake nodded energetically. "Also I told three kids that you are totally going to crush this class. No pressure."

"Jake," Emma groaned.

"Okay, maybe a tiny bit of pressure," he said.

Riley appeared and swatted Jake lightly with her glove. "Leave her alone. You are making her more nervous."

Jake grinned. "Pretty sure her nerves reached maximum capacity fifteen minutes ago."

Riley pointed at him. "Go. Somewhere. Far away."

Jake sprinted off, laughing.

Riley turned to Emma. "He is not wrong. You do look nervous. But you are also doing well. Keep Willow walking until they call your class."

Emma nodded gratefully.

Moments later, the announcer crackled through the speakers. "Walk trot beginners, please make your way to the main arena gate."

Emma's stomach dropped.

Marlene stepped close. "I will walk with you to the gate."

Emma nodded, her throat tightening.

Riley leaned in. "You have this. Just trust her."

Emma nodded again.

She mounted Willow with a deep breath, hands shaking slightly as she picked up the reins. Willow shifted once, then stood still as if sensing Emma's need for stability.

They approached the arena gate. A line of nervous beginners

waited on their horses. Some bounced in the saddle. Some whispered to their horses. A few looked like they might faint.

Emma fit right in.

When it was their turn, the gate steward smiled. "Go ahead."

Emma nudged Willow forward.

They entered the show arena.

The sunlight hit the sand in bright flashes. The banners fluttered along the fences. Parents and riders filled the chairs. The judge watched with calm focus.

Emma felt like the world was watching her.

She breathed deeply and whispered, "We can do this."

The class began.

The judge asked for a walk on the rail. Willow responded smoothly, ears flicking but body steady. Emma's nerves eased a little as she settled into the movement.

They made it through the first two laps. Then the judge called for a trot.

Emma's heart jumped.

She squeezed gently. Willow lifted into a trot with a quick step that made Emma wobble slightly. She caught her balance just in time, focusing on the rhythm.

Posting. Sit. Rise.

She matched Willow's stride, adjusting until everything clicked.

Halfway through the trot lap, a sudden burst of static exploded from the speakers.

Willow jolted hard.

Emma gasped and grabbed for her reins.

Willow sidestepped sharply, her neck tense, eyes wide.

Emma leaned forward instinctively and whispered in a low, steady voice, "Easy. Easy. I am here."

Willow trembled but did not bolt.

The judge waited calmly while the riders regained order.

Emma breathed, slow and deep.

Willow hesitated, then softened slightly.

When the trot continued, Emma kept her energy quiet and her mind focused. Willow eased back into the rhythm, still tense but trying.

When the class ended, Emma walked Willow out of the arena with shaking legs. Marlene met them with a bright, reassuring smile.

"You did beautifully," Marlene said. "You handled that spook perfectly."

"I thought she was going to bolt," Emma whispered.

"But she did not," Marlene said. "Because of you."

Riley appeared behind her, arms crossed but expression soft. "That was impressive."

Emma blinked. "Really."

"Yes," Riley said. "She tested you. You stayed with her. That is what matters."

Jake arrived seconds later, completely breathless. "Emma. You survived. I am so proud. That static noise almost made me fall over and I was not even riding."

Emma laughed shakily. "It was scary."

"But you stayed on," Jake said. "Which means you are officially a rider."

Emma exhaled, all the tension flooding out.

The class results were posted twenty minutes later.

Emma blinked at the paper.

She had placed third.

Not first. Not last.

Exactly enough to feel like a small miracle.

She hugged Willow's neck, overwhelmed with joy and disbelief. Willow breathed softly into her hair, calm and proud.

As Emma stepped back, Riley approached and nodded toward the ribbon. "Good job."

Emma smiled. "Thank you."

Riley hesitated for a long moment, then added quietly, "Willow chose you for a reason. Do not forget that."

Emma felt her heart lift. "I will not."

Jake slung an arm over her shoulders. "Come on, champion. There are cupcakes at the snack table."

Emma rolled her eyes. "You just want food."

Jake grinned. "Absolutely."

As Emma walked toward her parents, Willow safe in her stall behind her and a ribbon in her hand, she realized something important.

She could do this.

She could ride. She could trust Willow. She could trust herself.

And for the first time since moving to Saddle Creek, Emma felt like she truly belonged.

Chapter Eleven

The hours following Emma's first show class passed in a blur of movement, color, excitement, and noise. Her third place ribbon hung from her fingers, the fabric catching tiny flashes of sunlight as she walked back toward the barn with Willow by her side. Every part of her buzzed with pride. She felt taller somehow, steadier inside, as though she had finally taken a step into a world she had always admired only from the outside. Riders around her congratulated one another, parents hugged their kids, instructors called reminders, horses whinnied impatiently for hay or attention. Yet through all the bustle, Emma felt something clear and calm glowing in her chest. She had done it. She and Willow had done it together.

Willow walked with a relaxed stride, her ears softly swiveling as she took in the sounds of the show. She looked far less tense than she had in the warm up arena. Emma stroked her neck gently. "You were incredible today," she whispered. "You were scared, and you stayed with me. I promise I will try to be brave for you too."

Willow flicked an ear in her direction as if she understood every word.

When they reached the barn, Emma saw her mom and dad waiting near the aisle, both smiling broadly. Her mom clapped her hands together, her eyes bright with emotion. "Emma, you were wonderful." Her dad placed a hand on her shoulder and leaned in to whisper, "You looked like you belonged out there."

Emma felt heat rise in her cheeks. She smiled shyly and glanced at Willow, who sniffed her mother's hand with delicate curiosity. "It was scary for a second," Emma admitted. "But Willow listened. And somehow we made it through."

Riley appeared near the saddle racks, her expression guarded but not unfriendly. She seemed to hover at the edge of the aisle, watching quietly. Emma caught her eye and offered a small smile. Riley returned it with the tiniest nod before turning away. It was barely a gesture, but Emma felt its weight. Coming from Riley, even a nod felt like progress.

Jake jogged up moments later, out of breath and holding two cupcakes in one hand and what looked like a lopsided fruit cup in the other. "Victory snacks," he announced triumphantly. "One is for you. The other is for me. But I can be persuaded to share the fruit cup if you tell me you are allergic."

Emma shook her head, laughing. "Thanks, but I am fine."

Jake pretended to look offended. "Are you rejecting my gift."

"Only the fruit cup," Emma said. "Cupcakes are always welcome."

Jake grinned, handing one over. "This one has purple sprinkles. It looks like Willow."

Emma looked at it and blinked. "How does purple look like Willow."

Jake shrugged. "It is a vibe."

Emma giggled again. "Thank you."

The barn bustled with riders preparing for their next classes. Horses stood in grooming stalls while braids were tightened, hooves polished, tack adjusted, jackets brushed free of dust. Emma watched everything with a sense of awe. She had always dreamed of being part of this world. Now she was actually living it.

Marlene approached with a clipboard and a soft smile. "Emma, Willow looked wonderful out there. I know the static scared her, but you handled it with calm maturity."

Emma felt her chest warm at the praise. "It was scary. But I just kept thinking about my breathing. And about how I could not panic because then she would panic."

"That is exactly the mindset you want," Marlene said. "That is partnership. And today you proved you have one."

Emma stroked Willow's neck, feeling the mare's steady breath move beneath her fingertips. "She did most of the work."

Marlene shook her head kindly. "No. You both did."

For a moment, Emma felt like her heart might burst. She had heard compliments before, but none that seemed to reach so deep.

As she began untacking Willow, Riley stepped closer. She stood with her arms crossed, but her posture was less defensive today. "Your line in the corner during the trot was pretty good," Riley said.

Emma looked at her in surprise. "Really."

"Yes," Riley said, her tone slightly clipped as though giving praise was physically difficult. "You kept her steady even when she started to drift. That is not easy."

"Thank you," Emma said softly.

Riley pursed her lips. "Do not let it go to your head."

Jake whispered off to the side, "That is Riley speak for 'I am proud of you.'"

Riley whipped her head toward him. "I did not say that."

Jake held up his hands. "I know. I am reading between the lines."

"Stop reading between my lines," Riley snapped.

Emma bit her lip to keep from laughing.

Willow raised her head and nudged Riley gently in the arm. Riley stiffened in surprise. Willow nudged her again.

Jake clutched his chest dramatically. "She likes Riley today. The apocalypse is coming."

Riley glared at him but reached out slowly to touch Willow's forehead. The mare leaned into the touch, her eyes softening.

"See," Emma said. "She likes you too."

Riley's expression softened, her voice quiet. "Sometimes."

Emma almost said something more, something encouraging, but Marlene called for the next warm up group. Emma's class was over, but she knew she wanted to keep Willow active and calm. She brought her mare back to the stall where the air was cooler and quieter.

She brushed Willow slowly, enjoying the comforting rhythm. Willow leaned her head into Emma's shoulder, her warm breath brushing the back of Emma's neck. Emma stood still for a moment, letting the connection wash over her. "I am so lucky," she whispered. "I never thought I would get to ride someone like you."

From the end of the aisle, the announcer's voice drifted through the speakers. "Attention riders. The walk trot pleasure class will begin in twenty minutes."

Emma stiffened. "Walk trot pleasure," she murmured. She had signed up for that too. She almost forgot. She peeked at her schedule, her heart skipping. Yes. She was riding in it.

Marlene approached again. "Are you up for one more class today."

Emma hesitated. "I do not know. I am still nervous."

"That is understandable," Marlene said. "It is your choice. You do not have to enter. But if you want to keep building confidence while you are already warmed up, this is a good opportunity."

Emma stared at Willow. The mare's dark eyes watched her calmly, full of a soft intelligence that always felt like a whispering invitation.

"I want to try," Emma said quietly. "I think I should try."

Marlene nodded with a smile. "Then let us get her ready again."

Emma saddled Willow once more, careful and steady. The mare shifted once but remained calm. As Emma tightened the girth,

Willow turned her head and pressed her muzzle against Emma's shoulder.

Her nerves melted a little.

Jake arrived at the grooming stall, his face streaked with crumbs from a cookie. "Round two for the champion."

"I am not a champion," Emma said softly.

"You are today," Jake said with a grin. "Champions show up twice."

Emma rolled her eyes but felt a rush of warmth inside.

Riley stood a few feet away, adjusting a younger rider's gloves. When she finished helping, she looked over. "Good luck."

Emma blinked. "Thank you."

Riley nodded once, her posture stiff as if she was not used to saying it. Emma appreciated the effort.

Marlene motioned. "Time to warm her up again."

Emma led Willow to the warm up arena. This time Emma felt her fear differently. It was still there, a quiet trembling inside her stomach, but something else stood taller beside it. Familiarity. Trust. Willow's calm steps reassured her. The mare looked around but did not spook. Her ears flicked but did not pin. Her tail swished lazily. She seemed more confident than earlier.

Emma placed her foot in the stirrup, mounted, and gathered her reins. Willow breathed out, a long and peaceful exhale.

"You ready," Emma whispered.

Willow took a step forward, steady and smooth.

The warm up was busy again. Riders called out directions to avoid collisions. Horses circled. Dust rose in soft clouds. But this time Emma found her place in the chaos more easily. She walked Willow along the rail, letting her see everything. Then she trotted gently, matching the mare's stride.

Riley watched from the fence for a while, her gaze evaluating but thoughtful. When Emma passed her, Riley called out, "Shoulders back. She respects you more when you look confident."

Emma straightened her posture. Willow's ears turned back toward her as if noticing the difference.

"Better," Riley called.

Emma smiled.

Jake jogged past with two water bottles, panting. "You are dazzling out there," he gasped dramatically. "Now I must hydrate the masses."

Emma shook her head fondly. "Go, Jake."

After warming up for several minutes, Emma felt ready.

The announcer called her class to the gate.

She rode Willow toward the entrance, heart pounding but steady. She lined up behind two older riders who looked calmer than she felt. Willow lowered her head slightly, breathing deeply in a way that made Emma mimic her. She exhaled slowly.

"It is okay," she whispered.

The gate steward opened the arena door. "Riders, walk on the rail please."

Emma entered second. Willow stepped into the bright sunlit arena with slow, confident strides. For a moment, the world sparkled around them. Parents in the stands adjusted their cameras. Riders waiting for their turn peered through the rails. Banners fluttered lazily along the arena fence.

Emma sat tall, guiding Willow toward the rail.

The judge raised her clipboard. "Walk please. Riders, show me a relaxed horse."

Emma let her reins soften. Willow stretched her neck downward, relaxing beautifully.

Marlene, watching from the side, nodded in approval.

The judge seemed to notice too. She made a quick note.

Emma's heart lifted.

"Riders, please reverse through the diagonal."

Emma turned Willow gently onto the diagonal line. The mare moved willingly beneath her, smooth and focused.

"Very nice," Marlene murmured.

"Riders, trot please."

Emma squeezed lightly. Willow picked up a calm trot. The movement felt more balanced than the earlier class. Emma focused on her posting rhythm and breathed steadily. Willow's ears flicked, listening closely.

They trotted past the judge. Emma's heart thudded, but she kept her eyes up and her posture steady.

The judge nodded.

Emma exhaled.

They completed a few more laps. Everything felt natural. Trusting. Connected.

When the class ended, Emma walked Willow to the lineup. Her legs shook slightly from adrenaline. The judge approached the riders with a stack of ribbons.

"In first place," the judge announced, "number twenty seven on Skyline."

A tall rider on a bay gelding beamed as she accepted her blue ribbon.

"In second place," the judge said, "number fifteen on Willow."

Emma's mouth fell open.

Marlene clapped from the rail.

Jake whooped so loudly a nearby horse spooked.

Riley smiled, a real one this time, small but genuine.

Emma felt tears gather in her eyes. She leaned down and hugged Willow's neck tightly. "You are amazing," she whispered. "Absolutely amazing."

Willow flicked an ear and breathed warmly into Emma's leg.

Emma accepted her red ribbon with shaking hands. The color shone in the sunlight, bright and bold. She held it tightly as she left the arena.

Her parents met her near the barn, their smiles wide.

"You were wonderful," her mom said.

"You looked like you belonged out there," her dad added.

Emma felt a warmth spread through her from head to toe.

Inside the barn, she untacked Willow with careful, loving hands. Quietly, thoughtfully, she brushed the mare until Willow gleamed. Willow leaned into her touch, breathing deeply.

"You did so well," Emma said. "I cannot believe we placed second. You did that. You carried me."

Willow nickered softly, touching her forehead to Emma's shoulder.

Jake hurried over, nearly tripping on a broom. "Emma. You are practically a legend. People were whispering things like Who is that girl on the chestnut and Does she ride here often."

Emma laughed. "Jake, stop."

"I am serious," Jake said. "You were amazing."

Riley approached slowly. She looked at Willow, then at Emma. "You earned that ribbon," she said. "I am not just saying that. Your position was good. Your reins were soft. Willow respected you."

"Thank you," Emma said. "Really."

Riley nodded thoughtfully. "And you looked calm. Even when you were terrified."

Emma laughed. "Thanks. I tried."

Riley stepped closer to Willow and stroked her neck softly. "I think she is happy today."

Emma nodded. "Me too."

The barn bustled around them as the show continued, but for a moment the world felt quiet and still. Emma brushed Willow's coat, Riley stood by her side, and Jake told an exaggerated story about accidentally knocking over a stack of folding chairs earlier.

As the last classes of the day wound down, Emma walked Willow outside to graze. The late afternoon sun painted everything in warm gold. The air smelled like grass, warm earth, and the faint sweetness of the snack table frosting.

Willow cropped at the grass peacefully.

Emma studied the mare's calm posture, the way she chewed slowly, the gentle swish of her tail.

"We did it," she whispered.

Willow flicked an ear.

Emma closed her eyes for a moment and listened to the soft rustle of leaves, the gentle grazing noises, the distant murmur of voices. This place felt like home. These people felt like the beginning of her story. And Willow felt like a piece of her heart she had only just discovered.

When she opened her eyes again, the forest at the far edge of the property seemed darker than usual. A faint sound drifted from deep within, a soft, lonely cry that pricked at her senses. It made her think of the mysterious noise she had heard for days.

Willow lifted her head, ears turning sharply toward the woods.

Emma swallowed.

Something was inside those trees.

Something small.

Something scared.

And somehow, she felt that Willow knew more about it than she could say.

But that mystery belonged to another day.

Today belonged to Emma and Willow.

Today, they shone.

Chapter Twelve

The sunlight had begun drifting toward late afternoon when the last of the show classes wrapped up. A warm glow settled across the Saddle Creek property, softening the white fences and turning them honey colored. Riders gathered near the scoreboard to claim their ribbons, parents snapped photos beside the barns, and volunteers began stacking discarded cones and ground poles along the side of the arena. The energy that had hummed all day began to settle, turning from excited to content, the way a room feels after a successful party.

Emma stood beside Willow in the paddock area, her chest still fluttering with the lingering thrill of everything that had happened. Two ribbons hung from her bag, one red and one yellow, and each time she caught a glimpse of them her heart tripped all over again. She had not expected to earn anything. She had come into the day hoping only to survive the experience without embarrassing herself or Willow. Instead, she had discovered something inside herself she had never quite felt before. A bravery that was not loud or perfect, but steady and real.

Willow grazed quietly beside her, head lowering and lifting with the calm confidence of a mare who had done something meaningful. Her coat shimmered in the afternoon light. Her tail swished lazily at the flies. Every now and then she nudged Emma's sleeve as if reminding her that this moment belonged to both of them.

Emma gave her a soft pat. "You were amazing today," she whispered. "I hope you know that."

Willow flicked her ears and continued grazing. It made Emma smile.

Her mom and dad walked toward her from the stands, both wearing the same proud expressions they had carried since her second class. Her mom waved excitedly, the sleeve of her sweater flapping. "We have been looking everywhere for you. Your dad insisted we buy lemonade from the snack table and then spilled half of it on his shoes."

"I did not spill it," her dad protested. "Gravity betrayed me."

Emma laughed. The sound felt light and free. She hugged them both tightly. "Thank you for being here."

Her mom cupped Emma's cheeks. "We would not have missed it for anything. You looked beautiful out there."

Her dad nodded vigorously. "You looked strong too. Confident. You handled that spook better than I would have handled stepping on a Lego."

Emma grinned, warmth flooding her. "Thanks. It really helped knowing you were watching."

Her parents stepped back as Marlene approached from the aisle, clipboard tucked under her arm but her smile soft. "Emma," she said, "you and Willow were a highlight for me today. I am proud of how you handled every moment. The calm ones, the scary ones, and everything in between."

Emma felt her heart swell. Praise from Marlene always felt like a rare gem. "Thank you. You taught me everything."

"No," Marlene said, shaking her head. "You learned everything. I simply opened the door."

Willow lifted her head from the grass and blew warm breath into

Marlene's sleeve. Marlene chuckled and scratched gently under the mare's jaw. "You did good too, girl."

A few seconds later, Jake sprinted toward them, his show tie hanging crookedly again and his show coat unbuttoned. He skidded to a stop in front of Emma, bending over dramatically while panting. "I have news," he gasped. "Important news."

Emma raised an eyebrow. "What happened. Did you knock over another stack of chairs."

Jake pointed a shaky finger at her. "That was one time."

"Twice," Riley's voice said behind him.

Jake spun around. "You did not have to bring that up."

Riley approached calmly, her expression softer than it had been all day. Her dark show jacket was dusted with a few stray bits of hay, and her bun sagged slightly at the sides, as though the long day had finally worn it down too. "Your tie is crooked again," she said bluntly.

Jake groaned. "I know. It is cursed."

"Or you are careless," Riley said.

Jake placed a hand over his heart. "Wounded. Deeply."

Riley ignored him and turned toward Emma. "You did well today," she said. The words came out stiff at first, but not unfriendly. More like she was unused to forming them.

Emma offered a small smile. "Thank you. And thank you for your advice earlier. It actually helped a lot."

Riley blinked, surprised. "It did."

"Yes," Emma said. "When I straightened my shoulders, Willow listened better."

Riley glanced at Willow with thoughtful eyes. The mare raised her head again and looked at Riley directly. Riley's posture softened as she reached toward Willow's muzzle hesitantly. Willow stepped forward and nudged her palm.

Emma watched them quietly. There was something different this time. Not competitive. Not tense. Something like understanding.

"She missed you today," Emma said softly.

Riley's eyes flicked back to her, guarded again. "She did not."

"She did," Emma repeated.

Riley looked down. "Maybe I missed her too."

The words were barely audible, but Emma heard them. Jake heard them too, judging by the way his eyebrows shot upward and his jaw fell open.

"Riley, was that vulnerability," he gasped dramatically.

Riley smacked his arm. "Would you stop."

Jake yelped but grinned.

Emma stepped back, allowing Willow to graze again. Her parents walked toward the bleachers to get a better view of the awards table being dismantled. Marlene moved toward a group of younger riders who needed guidance, leaving Emma with Jake and Riley.

Riders passed them carrying ribbons or water bottles, chatting excitedly about how their classes went. The warm, sunlit chaos of Saddle Creek was comforting. It felt like a place where people belonged, a place where hard work and courage showed even in the smallest gestures.

Jake plopped onto a patch of grass beside Willow and stretched his legs out dramatically. "I give today ten out of ten stars," he said. "Actually eleven, because you got ribbons and I got cupcakes."

Emma sat down beside him. "What did you want to tell me earlier."

"Oh," Jake said, snapping his fingers. "Right. Your parents heard people talking in the bleachers. Apparently one of the show volunteers said you have a natural way with Willow. Something about your energy matching hers perfectly."

Emma's cheeks reddened. "She said that."

Jake nodded vigorously. "Lots of grown ups were impressed. And Coach Lennox from that fancy neighboring stables saw you ride too. She told someone that Willow looked more confident than she has seen her in months."

Riley's eyes narrowed slightly. "Coach Lennox saw Willow."

"Yep," Jake said. "She said this barn is getting better with every show."

Riley lifted her chin slightly, pride glowing through her stubborn posture. "Well. Of course she said that. Saddle Creek is the best."

Jake rolled his eyes. "You can drop the modesty act any time."

Riley ignored him.

Emma leaned her head against Willow's shoulder, feeling warmth radiate through the mare's coat. "I still cannot believe today happened."

"You earned it," Jake said. "And you were brave. That is important."

Emma looked up at him. "I do not think I was brave. I was terrified."

"That is exactly why you were brave," Jake said, shrugging. "Bravery is doing something even when you are scared. People who are not scared do not need to be brave."

Riley glanced sideways at Emma. "You stayed on during a spook. I have fallen off for less. That takes guts."

Emma blinked. "Really. You fell off."

Riley looked offended. "Yes. Riders fall. All riders."

Jake nodded enthusiastically. "I fall once a week."

Riley glared at him. "You trip on air."

"Air is sneaky," Jake muttered.

Emma laughed again, her stomach warm with joy. She had not expected to end the day with these two. But somehow it felt right.

"Do you think Willow liked showing," she asked softly.

Riley studied the mare. "Maybe. She trusts you. She is calmer when she trusts her rider."

Jake nodded. "Plus she looked cute with her braids. Very important."

Emma smiled. "She did look cute."

Willow lifted her head suddenly, ears flicking sharply toward the distant tree line. Her entire posture changed, alert but not frightened. Emma followed her gaze.

The forest at the edge of the property sat in deepening shadow as the sun dropped lower. The tall pines rustled gently in the wind.

Somewhere within the trees, something shifted. Emma felt a faint prickle at the base of her spine.

"What is she looking at," Jake asked.

"Probably nothing," Riley said quickly, though her eyes narrowed with curiosity. "A bird. A squirrel. Something small."

Emma continued staring. Beneath the drifting wind, she heard something faint. Very faint. Like a soft cry swallowed by distance. She had heard it before. Twice at night. A lonely, high pitched sound that tugged at her chest. Now she was certain she had not imagined it.

Willow stepped closer to the fence, her head high.

Emma swallowed. "I have heard something from the woods the last few nights."

Jake sat up straight. "Like what."

"I do not know," Emma said. "A cry. A small one. Not a bird."

Riley frowned. "Coyotes sometimes come close to the property."

"This did not sound like a coyote," Emma said. "It sounded like a baby animal."

Riley's eyes flickered. "Like a fawn maybe."

Emma shook her head. "I do not think it was a deer. It sounded more like a foal."

Jake's eyes widened. "A baby horse. Loose in the woods."

"That is not possible," Riley said quickly. "We would know if any foals were missing."

Emma shrugged. "I just know what I heard."

Willow continued staring at the woods, ears fixed forward. Something about her posture told Emma that Willow understood more than any of them.

The sound came again, barely audible, carried on a softer breeze this time.

Emma felt her heart thump.

Jake shivered. "Okay. That makes my spine feel weird."

Riley crossed her arms. "Probably an injured animal. This area has wildlife."

Emma nodded, though uncertainty swirled inside her. "Maybe."

Willow blew through her nostrils, sharp and focused. Emma rubbed her neck soothingly. "It is okay, girl."

Jake leaned close. "We should go investigate."

"No," Riley said immediately. "Absolutely not. It is getting dark and the forest is huge. You two will get lost."

Emma bit her lip. "I was not planning to go alone. I was just noticing the sound."

"Well notice it from here," Riley said firmly. "Barn rule number one. No wandering into the woods without an adult."

Jake sighed dramatically. "Fine. But I will be thinking about woodland creatures all night now."

Riley shot him a look that said stop talking.

Emma stepped closer to Willow again and stroked her cheek. The mare leaned into the touch, her worry easing. The soft pressure of Willow's forehead against Emma's palm grounded her, steadying her thoughts.

She exhaled slowly. "You are right. We should not do anything now."

Riley nodded, almost relieved. "Good."

Marlene returned a few minutes later with her arms full of left-over ribbons. "The judge said Willow looked lovely. And Emma, she said your soft hands were excellent."

Emma's cheeks warmed. "Thank you."

"Are you three heading home soon," Marlene asked. "It is almost time for the last clean up."

Jake groaned. "You mean the mountain of trash bags behind the snack tent."

Riley raised an eyebrow. "You are helping."

Jake groaned louder.

Emma laughed quietly. "I can help too."

Marlene smiled. "Only if you want to. You have done enough today."

Emma looked at Willow again. "I think I have a little energy left."

They walked together to return Willow to her stall. The mare stepped inside, turned to face Emma, and rested her nose gently against her chest. Emma closed her eyes, soaking in the gesture. She hugged Willow's neck softly. "I love you," she whispered.

Willow breathed warmly against her shoulder.

Emma felt tears prick her eyes. Happy tears. Grateful tears. She had found something here. Someone. She had found Willow. And that meant everything.

After settling Willow with fresh hay and water, Emma joined Riley and Jake in picking up discarded cups, ribbons, lost gloves, and snack wrappers. They worked slowly, laughing at Jake's exaggerated reactions to sticky trash and Riley's attempts to maintain her strict reputation while clearly enjoying herself.

As the sun slipped lower, painting the world in deep orange, the three of them stood together near the paddock fence. The field stretched out before them, the forest beyond whispering quietly.

"You know," Jake said, kicking a pebble lightly, "you two make a pretty good team."

Riley glanced sideways at Emma. "I guess we do."

Emma smiled. "I am glad we are not enemies anymore."

Riley scoffed. "We were never enemies. I was just annoyed."

Jake nodded. "That is Riley speak for 'I like you now.'"

Riley slapped his arm. "Stop translating me."

Emma laughed, feeling her heart warm.

The wind rustled through the leaves again, carrying another soft cry from deep within the trees. Emma stiffened. Willow, even from inside her stall, lifted her head sharply.

Jake and Riley paused.

"There it is again," Emma whispered.

Marlene stood near the barn entrance, looking toward the woods with a frown. "I have been hearing that too," she said. "I will check it out tomorrow with Mr. Harris. Could be an injured animal."

Emma nodded, feeling a ripple of anticipation.

A story was beginning there, in the shadows of the trees.

But for now, she leaned against the fence beside Riley and Jake, the three of them watching the sun fade behind the pines.

She had feared she would never fit in when she first arrived at Saddle Creek. She had feared she would never belong.

But now she had Willow.

And she had Jake.

And, surprisingly, she was starting to have Riley too.

Most importantly, she had found a place that felt like a beginning instead of an ending.

Saddle Creek was home.

And tomorrow, the mystery in the woods would call again.

From Saddle Creek to You

Thank you for riding alongside Emma and Willow through their very first adventures at Saddle Creek Stables. If you felt your heart race during the show, smiled when Emma made new friends, or wished you could reach out and brush Willow's soft chestnut coat, then you have already become part of the Saddle Creek family.

But Emma's journey is only beginning.

There are secrets hidden around the barns, friendships that will grow and change, and horses whose stories are waiting to be heard. Every horse at Saddle Creek has a past. Every rider has something they are learning to face. And somewhere in the shadows of the forest, something small and frightened has been calling out in the night, hoping someone will listen.

In Book 2, Emma will discover that courage does not always look like ribbons or perfect rides. Sometimes courage is answering a cry in the dark, trusting your instincts when something feels wrong, and believing that even the smallest life deserves protection.

As you continue through the series, you will meet new riders, new horses, new challenges, and brand new mysteries. Emma will learn what it means to be truly responsible, to stand up for what is right, and to trust her bond with Willow even when things get tough. Friendships will be tested, loyalties will shift, and surprising allies will step forward from the most unexpected places.

You are invited to ride beside Emma through every hoofbeat and heartbeat.

The pastures are wide. The forests are deep. The mysteries are waiting.

Are you ready for the next ride?

Book 2: The Lost Foal Mystery.

With warm wishes,

Wren Willowbrook